Advance Praise for
Crossing the Pressure Line

"*Crossing the Pressure Line* has a heartfelt journey, a uniquely charming setting, and a hero you're sure to root for. What more could a reader want?"

—Dan Gemeinhart, author of
The Remarkable Journey of Coyote Sunrise

"*Crossing the Pressure Line* is a heart-warming, middle grade book whose story contains simple rules for a well-lived life. The story deals with topics such as the ability to bounce back in the face of loss or disappointment, empathizing with others, setting goals, pushing limits, trying new things, dealing with failure, and developing a powerful inner voice."

—Shana Draugelis, founder of *The Mom Edit*

"Laura Bird's *Crossing the Pressure Line* is a heartfelt novel about finding joy, purpose, and human connection, even while grieving those you've lost. Set in the distinctive Northwoods of Wisconsin, it is also a love letter to that area and all of the natural beauty, wildlife, and summer delights one finds there if lucky enough to visit."

—Lisl H. Detlefsen, author of
Time for Cranberries and other children's books

"*Crossing the Pressure Line* is a wonderful tale covering the spectrum of emotions. We loved the journey this story took us on and especially loved following Clare on her mission to catch her first musky in honor of her grandpa. We definitely recommend adding this to your reading list!"

—Dan and Jenn Donovan, founders/owners of Musky Fool Fly Fishing Company

"Through Clare and her love for her grandfather, Laura Bird illustrates how each person can react to death differently, based on many factors. She effectively portrays grief as a process that is not a straight line, and she offers suggestions for effective coping and understanding. This is an important book that educates about grief through Clare's engaging family story, while also providing hope for grieving youth and the adults in their life who care for them."

—Holly Farmer, MA, LMHC, Director of Bereavement Services for Center for Hospice Care, and Director of Camp Evergreen, Mishawaka, IN

"This beautiful book captures the essence of childhood summers and the formation of intergenerational family bonds. It is a warm and identity-affirming story and a must-read. Children everywhere will bond with Clare as she inspires readers to listen to their inner voice and believe in themselves. *Crossing the Pressure Line* is a great classroom read for upper elementary students and offers opportunities for rich discussion about friendship, developing self-esteem, having a growth mindset, and trying new things."

—Sylla Zarov, elementary school teacher and principal for more than 25 years

"I fell in love with all the characters and cheered them on every step of the way, especially Clare. I love how she challenged herself, found her resilience, and discovered what she was capable of! She set big goals and never got discouraged when they seemed out of reach."

—Katy Bloodgood Miller, Senior Director, Athleta Girl

"Laura Bird's first novel is a classic coming-of-age tale of thirteen-year-old Clare Burch. Through scrumptious detail and exquisite wording, Laura gets into the mind of her protagonist, and into the mind of the middle grade reader. The themes are universal, yet they feel new and fresh with the Midwest backdrop and outdoor references throughout the book. As a middle school teacher, I know my students will love this book, and I can already hear the robust classroom discussions about loss, family, friendship, goals, and self-discovery. This is the perfect addition for any middle school ELA classroom."

—Lisa Allaman, BS Spanish Education, MA Special Education, EdD Educational Leadership, English learner teacher with more than 20 years of experience

"I fell in love with Clare Burch. She has a tenacious spirit, determination, and a very tender heart. She truly exemplifies the magical Northwoods of Wisconsin in her experiences and in her passion for the outdoors. This is such an engaging book; I couldn't put it down!"

—Janie Geiger, owner of Janie's Custom Tackle and angler with more than 30 years of experience

Crossing the Pressure Line

Laura Anne Bird

OrangeHat
PUBLISHING

orangehatpublishing.com - Waukesha, WI

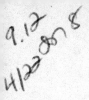

Crossing the Pressure Line
Copyright © 2021 Laura Anne Bird
ISBN 9781645382836
First Edition

Crossing the Pressure Line
by Laura Anne Bird

For information, please contact:

www.orangehatpublishing.com
Waukesha, WI

Cover Designer & Illustrator: Jayden Ellsworth
Art Director: Kaeley Dunteman
Editor: Jenna Zerbel

For Annie and William

She hated feeling sorry for herself,
but she couldn't help it.
Why do we get the life we're given?

—Kevin Henkes, *Sweeping Up the Heart*

If you were out in a great big woods with other trees all
around you and little mosses and Junebells growing over
your roots and a brook not far away and birds singing in
your branches, you could grow, couldn't you?

—L. M. Montgomery, *Anne of Green Gables*

I saw her do it, saw her reach down inside herself and find
strength. She was all kinds of strong.

—Dan Gemeinhart, *The Remarkable Journey*
of Coyote Sunrise

One
Something Big

At the end of the driveway, Clare Burch paused in front of her grandfather's peony bush, which was freshly, massively in bloom.

If only he were still here to enjoy it! she thought, eyeing the giant pink blossoms. *If only I'd heard Roger barking sooner! If only I'd been faster!* The if-onlys filled Clare's brain like useless pebbles. She shook her head and could hear them rattling around. She was sick of the sound.

It happened five months ago, and I'm still blaming myself. She wiped her nose with the back of her hand and wondered if things would ever get easier. *Not anytime soon*, she guessed.

The peonies were so hefty that they slouched right onto the grass. Roger snuffled the flowers with his little black snout while Clare held one in her hand, watching a few

1

ants purposefully wind their way around the petals. What adventures were they on? She wished she were as excited about something—*anything*—as they seemed to be.

Clare set the peony back down, substantial as a paperweight. For a fleeting second, she considered running back inside. She wanted to place her hand on Grandpa Anthony's urn and talk to it for a minute or two, but she was supposed to be meeting up with her best friends. She needed to tell them something—something big. The news had just been dropped into her lap like a package she couldn't quite wrap her arms around. She hoped Olive and Emmy would help her figure out a way to lift it.

It all started New Year's Eve.

Clare's eyes blinked closed, and the memory pressed in on her, as if someone were stepping on her toes or grasping her elbow too hard.

There was Grandpa Anthony, collapsed on the kitchen floor. His skin looked as gray as the grimy snow outside, and he was panting like Roger. He kept tapping his fingers, as if to get Clare's attention. "I'm here! I'm here, Grandpa Anthony!" she yelled, kneeling next to him. She reached into her sweatshirt pocket for her phone, but it wasn't there. She ran back upstairs to hunt for it, which was much harder than she expected because her legs were wobbling like crazy. Until she finally found her phone—which was tucked under her pillow—and dialed 911, every second that passed felt like a colossal, unforgiveable failure.

Roger barked, and Clare's eyes flew open. The bitter, white glare of winter instantly vanished.

"Sorry, buddy. Let's go," she said, but Roger was already trotting away on his stubby legs. As she followed him up the sidewalk, he zigged and zagged from the pavement to the grass and back again, just like a miniature brown rocket.

"Whose trail are you on? Maybe a rabbit's? Or a squirrel's?" Clare would never know for sure, but she envied Roger's sense of smell. She knew it was stronger than any human's—like one hundred or one thousand or even one million times as good.

Roger responded with a flip of his tail.

Clare held the leash taut so the pressure would keep him in something resembling a straight line. She looked ahead for fenceposts, rocks, and grooves in the sidewalk—anything he might collide with.

At the top of the street, she waved at her friends, who were coming from different directions. She noticed how happy they looked and felt sweat forming above her lip. She wished she didn't have to ruin their good moods.

"Yo," said Olive.

"Hiya," said Emmy. She bent down to rub the baby-fine fur under Roger's neck. "How's the best little blind dachshund I know?"

"He's the *only* little blind dachshund dog you know," said Olive.

"Oh, yeah." Emmy smiled and kissed Roger's smooth head. He nuzzled into her blond ponytail.

"So," said Olive, "what's this 'something big' you wanted to talk about?"

"Is Grandma Lulu forcing you to go to the spa with her again?" said Emmy.

"The last time she made you do that, you got slathered in mud!" shrieked Olive.

"No, that's not it." Clare shook her head. "And it was *purifying* mud, by the way. Whatever that means."

"It must be your mom, then," said Olive. "I bet she wants you and Grandma Lulu to mop the floors and organize the attic—all by tonight."

Clare sniffled, wishing desperately she had a tissue, and her friends stopped mid-laugh.

"Hey," said Emmy, "are you OK?"

"Yes. No." Clare tugged Roger's leash to keep him centered on the pavement. She could hear Grandpa Anthony's voice in her head. As they'd hurtled along in the ambulance, he had whispered in her ear: *Make it a great year. Make it a great life.*

"I don't know if I'm OK or not!" Clare whimpered.

Olive crossed her arms. "Tell us everything."

Clare opened her mouth, but her tongue was stuck. A hundred different words were waiting to be released, just like animals pacing in their cages. She had no idea which ones to set free first.

Emmy put her hand on Clare's arm. Her touch was

as light as the beating of a bird's wing. "Just start at the beginning."

Two
The Special Request

Clare took a deep breath. "Grandma Lulu got a phone call the other day." Her lungs released the air. "It was a lawyer. It turns out that Grandpa Anthony had a will, and it was pretty . . . specific. The lawyer's been going through all the details, and apparently, Grandpa Anthony made a special request."

"A special request?" said Emmy. "Ooh, that sounds intriguing."

"Grandpa Anthony said that whenever he died, he wanted his ashes to be scattered in the lake in Alwyn." *Hundreds of miles away, in northern Wisconsin,* she thought.

"Well, that makes sense," said Emmy. "He was from Alwyn. Maybe he just wanted to end up back home?"

Clare nodded.

"OK," said Olive, "go on."

6

Clare took another deep breath. "Well, Grandma Lulu's all upset now. She says she can't believe we have to dump him right in the water, with all the fish and the seaweed. She wishes that we could keep his ashes here in Chicago, because, according to her, he should be able to rest in peace in a marble mausoleum or something. You know, her idea of a civilized place."

Olive and Emmy rolled their eyes.

Clare herself wasn't bothered by the lake; she was more upset about emptying the urn in the first place. What would she do when the ashes weren't within reach, right on the mantle in the living room? How would she talk to Grandpa Anthony?

"No offense, but this special request doesn't sound like *that* big of a deal," said Olive, swishing her ginger hair. "I mean, I know it won't be fun, but you can do it, right?"

"Well, there's more." Clare licked the sweat off her lip. "Grandpa Anthony said that he wanted all of us to take his ashes up north. Me, Mom, and Grandma Lulu. He said that we need to spend the whole summer there. Living in the cabin. Together."

Olive gaped at Clare. "Wait a minute. *This* summer? Like, the one that starts in a few weeks? That's impossible. No way."

Clare nodded. Her shoulders would've sagged right off her body if she hadn't been responsible for walking Roger.

"You're saying that you're going to leave Morrissey and live in Alwyn for *more than two months*?" said Emmy. She was scrunching up her face so forcefully that Clare could count the wrinkles across her forehead: one, two, three. "But we've hung out every single summer since preschool!"

"I know," said Clare. "I like going to Alwyn for a *week*, but I can't imagine staying longer than that. Who will I hang out with? What'll I do on my birthday without you guys? I'll be turning thirteen with zero friends close by."

By now, Clare, Olive, and Emmy had walked all the way to the pool, which was located right in the center of their suburban neighborhood.

It's such a habit, thought Clare.

"Over here, you guys." She guided Roger over to the chain-link fence, and Olive and Emmy followed.

She stuck her nose through the steel wire, scrutinizing the scene of countless sun-soaked memories. The Morrissey pool was where she'd won ribbons at swim meets—and sometimes come in last place, too. It was where she'd devoured ice cream sandwiches, licking the treats from her fingers as they melted. It was where she'd played Marco Polo with Olive and Emmy over and over again, never tiring of their games. For as long as she could remember, the pool had centered her. She'd gotten fresh air and exercise there, and she'd discovered a deep sense of hard work and accomplishment.

"It's only for one summer," said Emmy. But they were such old friends that Clare knew Emmy was just trying to be positive for her sake.

"What about swim team?" said Olive. "How can you miss the entire season?"

Clare pressed her face harder into the fence. She knew she was making indentations across her cheeks, but she didn't care. "I don't know."

"Two months will go by fast," said Emmy, a minute later. "We can text each other all the time, and maybe Olive and I can visit."

"How will we do that, with swim practice every morning and meets on the weekends?" said Olive. "Our coaches will already be upset about losing Clare. They won't want you and me leaving town, too, Emmy."

Emmy threw her hands up. "OK, fine! Just don't forget that you love Alwyn, Clare. Doesn't that count for something?"

Emmy was right. Clare *did* love Alwyn. With its two glimmering lakes and regal trees that seemed to be high-fiving the clouds, Alwyn was a place where she'd always enjoyed herself. She had spent a week in their cabin every summer with her mom and Grandpa Anthony, and their vacations made her feel carefree and satisfied. Afterward, they'd return to their house in Morrissey, recharged and eager to jump back into regular life.

"Alwyn is great," said Clare, "but I can't imagine being

there—*living* there—for two months, without Grandpa Anthony. *He* was the main reason I loved going up north in the first place."

Grandpa Anthony had been born and raised in Alwyn. He'd known every bay, cove, and rock bar of Lake Alwyn and Lake Lyons—which, if you knew exactly where to look, were connected. His father had built their cabin by hand, using timber from their surrounding land. The walls were decorated with replicas of the biggest walleyes and smallmouth bass that Grandpa Anthony had caught. The bookcases were crammed with his old novels. And the kitchen counter was home to his permanently coffee-stained *Smile! I'm a Dentist!* mug. Clare sometimes thought of the cabin as a museum devoted to his life.

She sighed. "I don't know if being there will make me miss him more—or less. I can't stop thinking about all the little things. Like, who's going to take me to the bait shop? Who's going to buy me candy? Who's going to show me how to cast for muskies? Grandpa Anthony bought me a huge rod last year, before my hands were even big enough to hold it. He was going to teach me how to use it this summer."

"I guess it'll have to be your mom," said Emmy.

Clare and her friends burst into laughter.

"You're kidding, right?" said Clare.

"Yes," said Emmy.

"She hasn't painted anything since Grandpa Anthony died," Clare went on. "And since she won't be teaching her summer art classes here in Morrissey, she's worried that she'll never have a creative spark again. Which means she's crabby all the time. She won't want to do anything in Alwyn except be in a bad mood."

"What about Grandma Lulu?" said Olive, with a smirk. "Couldn't *she* take you fishing?"

"To be honest, I have no idea how Grandma Lulu will get through this summer." Clare wiped her eyes. She wasn't sure if her tears were from laughter or sadness—or maybe both. "Grandma Lulu *never* goes up north. Every time I've gone to Alwyn with Mom and Grandpa Anthony, she's stayed at home with Roger. You guys know she'd rather get a pedicure than hang out in nature."

Olive grimaced. "I definitely cannot picture her walking in the woods or shoving a fishhook through a worm."

"I can't either," said Clare.

"And Roger?" said Emmy, her face crestfallen.

"Yep," said Clare. "He's going, too."

"I hope he doesn't get eaten alive," said Olive.

"He won't get eaten alive!" Emmy jabbed her elbow into Olive's side.

Roger wagged his tail like a windshield wiper as he strained against his leash.

"When do you leave?" asked Olive.

"As soon as school's over," said Clare.

"Two weeks?" said Emmy, shaking her head mournfully. "That's unreal."

Roger had started to roll in the grass at Clare's feet. She reached down to brush the leaves and twigs from his fur. He smelled exactly like spring.

When she stood up, her friends draped their arms around her shoulders. Clare felt her muscles soften.

"It's going to be OK," said Emmy.

"I hope so." Clare didn't know whether to feel optimistic or pessimistic, or somewhere in between. "I guess I'll just have to be brave for once."

Olive and Emmy turned to face her. She avoided their gaze.

"You're the bravest person I know," said Emmy.

Immediately, Clare regretted bringing up the topic.

"Think of swim team," said Olive. "Even when a race is close and the crowd's going crazy, you never seem to get rattled. You do your thing, and you make it look easy."

"You might not be the biggest or the fastest one in the water, but your last laps are always as strong as your first," said Emmy.

"If that's not brave, I don't know what is," said Olive.

It's funny, how other people see me. Clare was relieved when a chipmunk scurried across the grass and sent Roger into a fit of yapping. Now they wouldn't have to talk about how supposedly courageous she was.

"Anyhow," Emmy went on, "I'm sad that you won't be around, but I'm excited for you."

"Me too." Olive tipped her head. "It's weird, having opposite feelings at the same time."

Clare was glad that her friends seemed to be as conflicted about her impending departure as she was. It made her change of plans a little easier to bear.

Roger wrenched away from the fence and began to scamper up the sidewalk in pursuit of the runaway chipmunk.

I'm just like a wad of play dough, thought Clare, running after Roger. *Stretched out in one direction, and then the other.*

"If nothing else, it'll be a big adventure!" yelled Emmy.

"Yeah, it'll be a big adventure for all of you!" said Olive.

Maybe, thought Clare, *but I'd rather have someone just stick me back in my little play dough can and close the lid.*

Three
The Size of a Shoebox

Within a few days, a tangle of boxes, bags, and suitcases littered the floors of the Burches' house.

"Good glory, it looks like a tornado blew through," Grandma Lulu grumbled as she gingerly picked her way down the hallway.

"You're just grumpy because you can't take every article of clothing you own up north with you," Clare's mom snapped.

"That's only *partly* true, Helen. I'm grumpy because I can't take all my shoes, either."

Clare went into her bedroom and flopped down between mounds of shorts and t-shirts. Packing for Alwyn was always a challenge: she needed clothes for chilly mornings and muggy afternoons, sweatshirts for roasting marshmallows at night, and multiple swimsuits so she never had to tug a wet one onto her body. Plus goggles, swim caps, and sneakers. Basically *everything*.

With a grunt, Clare smooshed her clothes in her duffel bag and then decided to pack a fleece and a flannel, too. She wanted to channel her inner Grandpa Anthony, because he'd always had the right gear for any situation.

"There's no such thing as bad weather, only bad clothing," she said, quoting him. She grabbed the extra clothes from her closet and added them to the duffel. Then she glanced at the tower of novels that practically came up to her waist.

As if reading Clare's mind from a room away, her mom shouted, "You're only allowed to pack a couple of books, Clare! Do *not* get it into your head that you can bring them all. You can't, or we'll never be able to fit everything in our cars!"

Clare scowled. She plucked *The Remarkable Journey of Coyote Sunrise* from the top of the stack and placed it between two pairs of leggings. Then she sat on her lumpy bag and bounced a few times. Heaving at the zipper, inch by inch, she managed to get it fastened.

Her mom yelled again. "Clare!"

Clare flinched.

"Remember, you have a card for the public library in Alwyn. You'll be able to ride your bike there and check out books anytime you want."

Laura Anne Bird

"OK, I get it!" Even though Clare loved libraries, she was seriously annoyed. Her mom was in full-on organizing mode, gathering up beach towels, bike helmets, and cans of insect repellent like they were weapons for an impending battle. Clare smiled to herself when her mom turned her attention to Grandma Lulu instead.

"You *cannot* go up north without decent footwear," her mom was saying.

"I believe that's a matter of opinion, Helen," said Grandma Lulu.

"Well, Mom, it's much easier to run from a bear when you're not wearing high heels."

"Did you say a *bear*?"

"I'm kidding, Mom. Relax."

"*You're* telling *me* to relax, darling? Oh, the irony."

Clare shook her head. She wondered how her mom and grandmother would get through an entire summer up north without strangling each other.

"Enough packing for now," she murmured. Downstairs, she wouldn't have to listen to anyone's bickering.

In the living room, Clare strode right over to the fireplace. She placed her hands on the mantle, on either side of the urn. "Hi, Grandpa Anthony."

The urn was polished and smooth, and its light-colored wood glowed as warm as toast. Grandpa Anthony's best friends in Wisconsin had made the urn by hand back in winter, just in time for his funeral service at St.

16

Kevin's. Nine inches long and five inches high—the size of a shoebox—it inconceivably contained what was left of the person Clare loved most in the world.

She wondered for the thousandth time how Grandpa Anthony had managed to get *in* there—the strong, broad-shouldered man who'd stood so tall. She understood that he'd been cremated, but that wasn't the point. How could someone who'd had such an imposing physical presence be sitting above the fireplace, like it was no big deal?

"I'm almost done with my packing." Clare's voice was a whisper, no louder than the breeze that drifted through the living room windows. She didn't want anyone to know that she talked to the urn like it was a real person. She worried that it made her look like she was silly, or babyish, or in denial. After all, Grandpa Anthony had been gone since winter. Shouldn't she be over it now?

"We're going to Alwyn next week, but don't worry, you're coming, too." She patted the urn. "Although I guess you know that already, seeing how you requested it. I just wish I knew why you wanted all three of us to go up north together, for two whole months. Why couldn't Mom and I have gone up for a week, like we normally do? Because now I have to miss swim team, and Mom can't teach any of her summer art classes. And obviously Grandma Lulu needs to be with us when we scatter your ashes, but she doesn't seem very happy about leaving Chicago."

What were you thinking, Grandpa Anthony?

"Anyhow, seventh grade is almost over. Last week, I turned in my research project for science class. It was about birds. We could choose whatever species we wanted. You'll never guess what I picked."

Clare looked at the urn expectantly, but it remained silent.

"I picked crows! Kind of random, since everyone else thinks they're obnoxious, but I was inspired by 'The Raven.' You know—the creepy poem by Edgar Allen Poe? I learned a bunch of stuff, and Mrs. Bergan told me I did an excellent job."

Clare thought about how much time she'd poured into her research. It had been nice to focus on something other than the sorrow and blame that had been chugging through her head like a train without a caboose.

Clare heard her mom and grandmother coming downstairs. "I gotta go now. Mom and Grandma Lulu have finished fighting, I guess." She blew her bangs off her forehead. "Seriously, I don't know how we're going to get by without you as the buffer between them. We've done OK so far, but that's only because Mom's been busy at school, and Grandma Lulu's been doing her usual social things."

She wished her grandfather's voice would emerge from the urn and tell her what to do, but the urn just sat there.

She swallowed.

"No friends, no swim team, no *you*, and a mom and grandmother who are experts at arguing."

But, as she turned away from the mantle, a little noise deep inside her head announced itself.

Just make it work, Clare Burch, said the voice.

Her ears perked up.

Make it work.

Four
The Departure

The morning after seventh grade ended, Clare woke up before her alarm buzzed. Instead of lying there and staring at the ceiling—which she'd done every day since winter—she jumped right out of bed.

Burrowing her toes in the carpet, Clare placed one hand on her stomach and the other on her chest. She felt the rise and fall of her lungs, the thumping of her heart, and the gurgling of her hunger. She didn't know what was in store for her in Alwyn. *But I'm all here, in one piece*, she thought.

Her mom knocked on the door and poked her head inside. "Rise and shine! We're leaving soon, and I've got a last-minute to-do list for you." She slapped a piece of paper on top of Clare's dresser and was gone before Clare could respond.

"Beware the taskmaster," she muttered.

Ever since Grandpa Anthony's lawyer had told them about the will, Clare's mom had been like a symphony conductor, waving an imaginary baton as she directed their organizing, cleaning, and packing. Clare got tired just thinking about it. She knew getting ready to leave was a lot of work, but if her whole summer was going to be like that, it wouldn't be any fun at all.

An hour later, Clare crammed the very last of her gear inside Grandpa Anthony's pickup truck, which Clare's mom had decided to drive instead of her old, beat-up car.

Helen climbed into the driver's seat and switched on the ignition, and Clare tried not to giggle. Her mom was so small, and the truck was huge; plus, her dyed fire-engine-red hair matched the car's glossy finish perfectly. It was as if they'd been spray-painted from the very same can.

Clare set Roger, who was nestled inside his carrier, in the back seat of Grandma Lulu's sleek, black sedan. Then she climbed into the front as she watched her grandmother flutter in and out of the house like a piece of confetti.

Things are always a little more entertaining when Grandma Lulu's around, thought Clare. Which was why she'd wanted to be her grandmother's copilot for the drive up north.

Helen drummed her fingers against the dashboard of the truck. She looked at her watch and rolled down the window. "Are you ready to go yet, Mom?" she shouted. "We were supposed to leave twenty minutes ago!"

"Yes, Helen, I'm ready to go," said Grandma Lulu as she got into her car. "First, I forgot my cell phone. Then I had to use the restroom, one last time. And *then*, I realized I hadn't grabbed my sunglasses, which are an *absolute necessity* because I refuse to drive three hundred and sixty-four miles without something to protect my eyes from dangerous ultraviolet rays."

Grandma Lulu pushed her aviators up the bridge of her nose and turned to Clare. "Good glory, your mother can be so tetchy sometimes."

"Tell me something I don't know," said Clare under her breath.

"All right, then. It's time to get out of here. Finally." Clare's mom pulled out of the driveway and started up the street. The plan was for Clare and Grandma Lulu to follow her for the six hours it would take to get to Alwyn.

"Goodbye, Morrissey. Goodbye, Olive and Emmy. Goodbye, pool and swim team," said Clare.

"Goodbye, beautiful house and five-star restaurants and civilization," said Grandma Lulu.

Clare reached over to wipe away the fat tear that was trailing down her grandmother's face.

They drove to the top of the block—until Clare clapped her hands to her cheeks so hard that she was afraid she'd left a bruise. "Oh my gosh, we forgot Grandpa Anthony!"

Grandma Lulu screeched as she slammed on the brakes. "Sacrilege!" She tooted the horn and yelled out the window, "Stop, Helen! We forgot your dad!"

Clare saw her mom put her head on the steering wheel and bang it a few times.

"I am the *worst* granddaughter." Clare's cheeks pulsed, either from the slap she'd given herself, or from embarrassment that she'd let her grandfather down, once again.

"Don't be ridiculous," said Grandma Lulu as she turned the car around. "Your mother and I didn't remember Anthony, either. You cannot take responsibility for this." She lowered her sunglasses and waggled her long eyelashes in Clare's direction.

Clare waggled her eyelashes back.

"We've been so busy stuffing two cars with rain boots and sun visors and dog treats, it's inevitable that we would forget something," said Grandma Lulu. "I'm just relieved that you remembered him before we were halfway to Wisconsin, darling."

Once they were back home, Clare sprinted into the noiseless house. "I'm so sorry we forgot you," she said to the urn, lifting it off the mantel. "We got caught up in our packing. It was a little harder without you in charge, but we figured it out."

Laura Anne Bird

Clare locked up the house for the second time. When she got to the passenger door of Grandma Lulu's car, she paused. She could see her distorted reflection in the black paint. Her head, with its straight, acorn-colored hair, looked unnaturally large. So did the urn in her arms. She could feel Grandma Lulu and her mom watching her, as if wondering what she would do next.

Is it weird that I want to keep the urn next to me?

She shrugged and climbed inside.

I don't have much longer with his ashes. If I'm a freak, then I guess I'm a freak.

She wrapped her seatbelt carefully around her own body, as well as the urn. It felt like she was buckling up for a big, unknown journey. The only thing she knew for sure was that the ashes wouldn't be coming back to Morrissey with her when the adventure was over.

She took a deep breath.

"Let's go to Wisconsin."

Five
Highway Eight

Grandma Lulu followed Helen north on the interstate, the traffic loosening as they disentangled themselves from the suburbs. Office buildings and shopping malls gave way to tidy parks and baseball fields, which morphed into lush farmlands and boxy red barns.

Clare read the sign out loud when they passed the state line. "*Welcome to Wisconsin!*" A solitary black crow coasted over the highway. She watched his dark body disappear behind a puffy cloud.

"We're making good time, aren't we?" said Grandma Lulu.

"Yep. We're officially in America's Dairyland now," said Clare.

"Would you grab my tote bag from the back seat, darling? I packed a little something for you."

Laura Anne Bird

Clare located the tote and rooted around inside, where she found hairbrushes, tubes of makeup, and a bottle of perfume. "Is she seriously planning on using all this stuff in Alwyn?" she whispered to Roger, who lifted his head in his carrier. She tried to stifle her laughter as she pulled out a crinkly bag of red licorice.

"Not that I ever tagged along on your road trips, but I remember your grandfather always saying that no drive up north was complete without candy," said Grandma Lulu.

Clare ripped open the bag with a gratifying tear. The syrupy smell of artificial strawberry rose into her face. "Ooh, thanks! It's the twisty kind!"

In the backseat, Roger whined.

"Not for you, buddy," she murmured, and he went back to his snoring. She unwound the licorice into mini strands, and she used the mini strands to make designs all over her arms. She created a sun with rays sticking out of it. And a boat. And a fish. She waved her arms so her grandmother could see.

"I'm glad that *someone* in this family is feeling creative," said Grandma Lulu, pursing her lips.

Clare frowned as she thought about her mom, and then she snorted the licorice off her arm like a piglet.

"What lovely manners you have!" said Grandma Lulu.

Clare laughed and began to feed stands of licorice to her grandmother as she drove. Together they finished off the bag, leaving their teeth red and sticky.

26

But then, out of nowhere, Clare felt a hot rush of panic. "Do you think it's OK that I'm having fun right now, Grandma Lulu?"

"Whatever do you mean?"

Clare listened to the hum of the tires on the road. "I still really, really miss Grandpa Anthony. But it's nice to be missing him on a road trip instead of hiding in my room and crying."

Grandma Lulu reached over to clasp Clare's hand. She kissed the back of it, leaving a perfect imprint of red lipstick. "I've felt like a pocket turned inside out since your grandfather died, and I'm not sure how I'm going to fill up the empty space inside of me. Eating fancy lunches downtown certainly hasn't worked. Same goes with manicures and tennis lessons. I've decided it's got something to do with going up north with you and your mom. Anthony wanted us to be doing exactly this. Which is a long-winded way of saying that yes, it's perfectly all right that you're having fun right now."

"I guess." Clare kissed the back of Grandma Lulu's hand, leaving a waxy trace of coconut lip balm. "I know that Grandpa Anthony loved Alwyn—and I do, too—but I still don't get why he wanted us to spend the whole summer there. I have no idea when I'll see Olive and Emmy again, and I can't celebrate my birthday with them. And I'm missing an entire season of swim team, so how am I supposed to stay in shape? And Mom can't teach her summer classes, and you'll literally be a state away from your hairdresser."

"Good glory, please don't remind me." Grandma Lulu brushed her platinum blond curls away from her face. "And yet . . . I wonder if maybe that's what this summer is all about."

Clare shrugged and watched the cow-dotted countryside roll by. Mile after mile, she felt herself moving farther away from what was familiar.

"I've got another present for you," said Grandma Lulu. "A little thirteenth birthday gift, a couple days early."

"More candy?" Clare smacked her lips. She was like her grandfather in that way: she would *never* turn down sweets.

"Absolutely not. You've had your sugar quota for the day, and I certainly hope you don't forget to floss tonight. Can you reach into the glove compartment?"

Clare unlatched the lock and peered inside. "*Charlotte's Web*? Why? I've already got my own copy."

"Take a closer look at it. That book is *old*. Practically an artifact! It was your grandfather's when he was a kid."

Clare smiled so widely that she could actually see her molars in the car's side mirror. They were still tinged red from the licorice.

"I found it in his nightstand when I was cleaning out some of his things. I remember him rereading it a year or two ago, although I never understood why he was so interested in a kid's book. Anyhow, I decided it needed a new owner. It needed *you*."

Clare held *Charlotte's Web* to her nose and sniffed. She was unaccountably disappointed that it didn't smell like Grandpa Anthony, but it did have the woody book-fragrance that she loved. "Thank you," she said, "so much."

Clare opened the cover of the book and gasped. On the first page, her grandfather had inscribed his name—not once, but twice: first in large, childish letters, and then in the blocky, grown-up handwriting she knew so well.

It was like she was getting two ages—two versions—of her grandfather in just one book. "Wow." She flipped through *Charlotte's Web*, which was dog-eared, underlined, and wonderfully scruffy.

"He was always fiddling with the pages of whatever he was reading, wasn't he?" said Grandma Lulu.

"Yep. He even underlined a couple things here in *Charlotte's Web*."

"Really? Why don't you read them out loud?"

Clare cleared her voice as she smoothed the page. "'The light strengthened, the mornings came sooner.'"

"How lovely."

"That describes summertime in Alwyn *exactly*."

"Well, if that's what summer up north is like, it doesn't sound so terrible. Maybe I'll survive, after all." Grandma Lulu gave a melodramatic shudder.

"It won't be that bad, Grandma Lulu." Clare laughed.

"That's easy for you to say! You know what you're getting into, whereas *I* haven't been to Alwyn in many, many years."

Clare tipped her head. It occurred to her that maybe she wasn't the only one feeling out of sorts. "Do you want me to read another line?"

Grandma Lulu nodded.

"'It is deeply satisfying to win a prize in front of a lot of people.'"

"Why would *that* sentence resonate with your grand-father? He never won a prize in front of a lot of people—to my knowledge, anyway."

"It's definitely a strange thing to underline." Clare went back to riffling through *Charlotte's Web*, and a small square of paper floated from the pages. "Check out his bookmark! It's a receipt from the supermarket for Tropical Chomps and Choco Crunches."

"He was a dentist who loved sweets," said Grandma Lulu. "Unbelievable."

How many times had Clare found his candy wrappers tucked around the house in odd places? It had been an ongoing joke between them for as long as she could remember. *I guess the joke is over forever*, she thought.

To fend off her tears, she focused her attention on the giant blue silos out her window, wondering what crops were stored in them. *There are so many things that people just can't see from the outside.*

Then she glimpsed a big green road sign. "We're almost to Tomahawk! Highway Eight is just ahead, Grandma Lulu!"

Grandma Lulu looked alarmed, as if she'd missed an exit ramp or forgotten to fill up the tank with gas. "I have no idea what you're talking about, darling! What in the world is Highway Eight?"

"The *pressure line* is coming up!"

"I *still* have no idea what you're talking about!"

"I guess you wouldn't know about the pressure line, since you've skipped all of our vacations up north," said Clare, not unkindly.

"Darling, for me a vacation consists of room service and a king-size bed with super-fluffy down pillows."

"Grandpa Anthony always said that Highway Eight, which is just past Tomahawk, is where up north officially begins," Clare went on. "Look ahead—do you see how the road goes from four lanes to two? It's like we're shifting into something new. He would always freak out when we drove across it. He'd start yelling, 'Feel it, Clare? Feel it, Helen? Breathe it in! The air's got more oxygen now! Forget about your worries. Just be present right here, right now!'"

Clare didn't think she could've adored her grandfather any more than in that particular moment.

"Do you believe it?" Grandma Lulu looked skeptical. "Do you really think there's a pressure line?"

"Sure, I guess." For the first time, Clare appreciated the idea of crossing from one thing into another. A different place. A different season. A different mindset. "It can't hurt to have faith in something like that."

As the four-lane highway tapered, Clare bounced in her seat. Grandma Lulu rolled the car windows all the way down, and Roger barked.

"Here it is!" shouted Grandma Lulu.

"Feel it? Breathe it in!" yelled Clare.

They inhaled extravagantly, and Clare swore that her skin grew a little pinker from the air, which *definitely* felt full of something, whether it was oxygen or some other magical Northwoods element. Grandma Lulu tooted the horn, and they waved crazily at Clare's mom. Helen turned her worried face to the truck's back window and lifted her hand as if to say, *"Don't you dare tell me we forgot something else."*

"We just crossed the pressure line!" shouted Clare.

She could see her mom's expression soften.

Helen gave a thumbs-up, and they all whooped.

But then the red brake lights flashed on the truck.

"Why's she slowing down?" said Grandma Lulu. "Why's she pulling off the road?"

"I have no idea," said Clare. "We're still an hour away from Alwyn, and Mom *never* takes detours."

Six
The Arrival

Clare and Grandma Lulu followed Helen off the highway and down a country road, not saying anything until Clare recognized their destination, with its white picnic tables and rainbow-striped umbrellas. "It's the Ice Shanty! Grandpa Anthony brought us here a few times, but it's been a while. I can't believe Mom even remembered where it was."

"I'm amazed that she's willing to waste precious time to stop and get a treat," said Grandma Lulu.

"I love it when she's in a good mood." Clare left the rest of her thoughts unsaid: *I just wish it happened more often.*

"The sign says they have the best frozen custard in Wisconsin. That sounds like a tall order to fill."

"My favorite thing to get here is two scoops of mint chocolate chip in a waffle cone, with chocolate sprinkles all over the top."

Grandma Lulu sighed as she pulled into the dirt parking lot. "There goes my figure for the summer."

Clare met her mom in front of the Ice Shanty and wrapped her arms around her.

Helen kissed the top of Clare's head. "I thought we could use a little break from all the driving."

"Do you think it's all right that I left Grandpa Anthony in the car?" whispered Clare. She had no idea what the rules were for toting an urn around in public.

"Of course."

"I feel like he should be here with us," said Clare. "Alive, I mean. He'd be sitting at that table over there—"

"—sucking down a strawberry shake with whipped cream," said Clare's mom. "Actually, that's what I'll get. In his honor."

Grandma Lulu joined them, holding onto Roger's leash. He scurried around their feet, sniffling the dandelions and sneezing from the dust. "I've given it some thought, and I've decided to order a turtle sundae, darlings. With extra caramel and pecans, naturally."

"Naturally." Clare grinned.

As she nibbled the sprinkles on her frozen custard, Clare looked back and forth between her mom and her grandmother. They were talking and laughing, and

Grandma Lulu even reached over to wipe a splotch of strawberry shake from Helen's chin.

I guess if I can't have Grandpa Anthony here, this isn't so bad, she thought.

It was so different from anything she'd ever known or envisioned, but she wondered if it could be just as good.

...

It was early afternoon when the Burches' two-car caravan rolled into the first small towns of the Northwoods: Hazelhurst, Minocqua, Woodruff, Arbor Vitae.

Clare announced their names as they drove through each one. She peered intently out her window at the gift shops, restaurants, and happy, sunburned people moseying along the main streets. Unlike every other summer, when she'd been a tourist herself, Clare felt different now. She wasn't a visitor anymore. This was going to be her actual home—for a couple months, anyway. She hoped she could figure out a way to belong.

"Look at that!" Grandma Lulu pointed. "Adler's Cheese Castle Café."

Clare thought of the luscious slabs of cheddar and pepper jack inside the shop, and her stomach rumbled.

"Stieghorst Pharmacy and Soda Fountain," Grandma Lulu continued. "I didn't even think you could find soda fountains anywhere anymore. Aren't they extinct?"

"I guess not." Clare picked up where Grandma Lulu left off. "Oscar's Brat Garden. Our Lady of the Tamaracks Church."

"Why, it's all so charming!"

"That's up north, Grandma Lulu."

"Would you believe that I felt like I was on a different planet the very first time your grandfather brought me to Alwyn?"

"Yes." Clare smiled and rubbed the urn like a lucky charm. "I would totally believe that."

"I know I've never really tried, but I wonder if I'll *ever* feel like I belong here," said Grandma Lulu.

Clare stared at her. "I was just wondering the same thing—about me, I mean. I guess we just have to give it our best shot. We'll be fine, no matter what." It was the little voice again, in the back of Clare's head, nudging her to say the words. She liked the sound of them.

A few miles later, Helen slowed the pickup truck.

Grandma Lulu slowed her car.

"It's just up ahead," said Clare. Through the stand of red pines along the road, which smelled just like Christmas, she could make out the cabin. She caught a glimpse of the thick, golden logs that had weathered more than a half-century on Lake Alwyn. She could see the tip of the A-frame and the grand stone chimney jutting out on top.

Grandma Lulu turned into the driveway, which was long and meandering and paved with pea gravel.

Clare closed her eyes and sniffed the spruce, ever-greens, and cedars that surrounded her like a band of protective friends.

The little rocks clattered against the car's wheel wells. The noise was as familiar to her as the sound of her own breathing.

The cabin sprawled before her, waiting, ready.

"Welcome home?" said Grandma Lulu.

"Welcome home," said Clare, her hands twitchy and damp.

As her grandmother eased the car into the garage next to the truck, Clare could barely keep herself from bolting out of her seat.

We're here, we're here, we're here.

She wanted to take it all in—the grass, trees, lake, dock, raft, and sky—and then she wanted to place her grandfather's ashes on the mantle in the great room, where he would have the very best view.

She felt like Roger being unclipped from his leash, because the moment that Grandma Lulu turned off the car, Clare—and the urn—were gone.

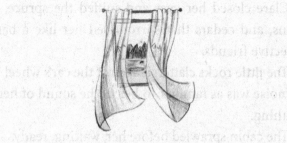

Seven
Three Goals

Her first night in Alwyn, Clare couldn't get her mind or her body to rest—even after reading for an hour. She made it halfway through *The Remarkable Journey of Coyote Sunrise* before placing it on her nightstand with a sigh.

Although she'd slept in the same bed every time she'd come up north, it suddenly felt foreign to her. On top of that, the energy in the cabin seemed like it was tuned to a new frequency. Her mom was in the small bedroom next to hers, and Grandma Lulu and Roger were in the loft upstairs, where Grandpa Anthony had always slept. Just switching around a few people and adding in a dog shook everything up.

Even though it was late, Clare texted Olive and Emmy.
I can't relax. :(

Count some sheep, said Olive. *Or blind dachshunds. Whatever! :)*

You'll be OK, I know it, said Emmy, adding in a line of hearts.

Hope so. Miss you guys.

Clare listened to the hum of the crickets and the *plink* of the waves against the dock, and after an hour or two, she finally drifted off to sleep.

It felt like only a few minutes had passed before her eyes flew open. "We have to go out fishing while the moon's still out!" she cried. As she kicked off her blanket, she wondered why Grandpa Anthony hadn't come in yet to give her an early-morning wake-up kiss.

But as her feet hit the knotty pine floor, she remembered that this trip up north was different than all the others.

"Oh." She put her head in her hands and felt the loss of him all over again. It was like a tension under her ribs, a perfect crescent of grief.

She wanted to jump back into bed and yank the covers over her head.

But the birds were singing, and slices of sunshine were beginning to emerge on her rug, and Clare decided that she wasn't going to lie around and feel sorry for herself. Summer needed to be completely different than winter and spring had been. *No more staring at the ceiling and sniffling. No more being so hard on myself.*

"It's my last day of being twelve," she announced to her little room. The walls were painted a robin egg blue that reminded her of the sky scoured clean after a rainstorm, and the gauzy white curtains curled and billowed as fresh air wafted through. She imagined they were happy to be dancing again after being still for so long.

She padded over to the window and thought about Grandpa Anthony's final words to her. *Make it a great year. Make it a great life.* He hadn't blamed her for anything when he died; instead, he'd been hopeful and reassuring—her own personal cheerleader.

Maybe I need to do what Grandpa Anthony always wanted, which is to be daring and brave and accomplish everything I can, she thought. *He'd want me to have faith in myself and just go for it—whatever 'it' is.*

She stared out at the lake.

Maybe I need to set some goals for myself while I'm in Alwyn.

Things that I can focus all my attention on—like the crow project I did for school.

Things that will help me feel like I belong.

Things that might even help me get through my sadness.

First, Clare thought about Olive and Emmy. No one would ever take the place of her two oldest friends, but she knew they didn't want her moping around all summer. They could text each other, for sure, but it wasn't the same as having real-live people to hang out with.

"Goal number one. I need to make a friend," said Clare to herself. "There must be kids my age in Alwyn. I don't know how I'll meet anybody, since I've only hung out with Mom and Grandpa Anthony when I've been here, but I can figure something out . . . right?" The thought of introducing herself to someone new made her feel jittery, like she'd just shoved too many strands of sugary licorice in her mouth. But she held up a hand, as if to stop her uncertainty from swallowing her in one piece.

Just make it work, Clare Burch.

Next, she thought about how she was missing swim team back in Morrissey. Without practice every morning, she needed something physical to do. "Goal number two. I will swim all the way out to the island and back"— she grabbed her phone from the dresser and did some quick math with the calculator—"in one hour or less." That seemed about right, considering her personal bests from the pool as well as the unruly nature of lake water. "Without wearing a life jacket!"

This goal felt big and bold, the sort of personal competition her grandfather would relish. He wouldn't be around to yell encouragement at her like he'd always done at swim meets, but she could learn to cheer for herself instead.

Couldn't she?

"It'll be hard, but I'll train by doing laps every day. I can swim back and forth between the dock and the raft, which is about the same length as the pool."

She eyed the caps, suits, and goggles that she'd brought with her from Morrissey. She was so glad she'd packed all of them.

Finally, Clare pictured the musky rod that Grandpa Anthony had bought her the year before. Unused and shiny—except for a few spider webs—it was still waiting in the garage. "I haven't had a huge growth spurt or anything, but I think I'm a little bigger now." She flexed her fingers and remembered how Grandpa Anthony had loved fishing for muskies, even though he'd never hooked one himself.

"Goal number three. I will catch a musky!"

She chewed her lip.

"I know it'll be super hard. There are people who go out every single day for months and never even see one, but I have to try. I mean, what's more incredible than catching a musky in Alwyn, the musky capital of the world?"

Clare liked the idea of striving for something important. *Three* things, actually. She hoped they would act like superglue and hold her together for the months ahead.

"I turn thirteen tomorrow," she said. "It's time to get started."

Laura Anne Bird

Eight
The First Morning

In the kitchen, Clare found that her mom and grandmother were up, too. She gave each of them a kiss and peered inside the virtually empty fridge. At least they had a jug of orange juice.

"I simply *cannot* abide the linens that Anthony had on his bed," Grandma Lulu was saying to Clare's mom. "They're as cozy as a piece of burlap."

"Well, what can we do about it? We're sort of roughing it this summer, remember?" Helen fiddled with Grandpa Anthony's elaborate coffee maker and made a wry face. "And yes, I realize the irony in saying this while trying to figure out how to use an Italian espresso machine."

"As a matter of fact, Helen, I've already taken matters into my own hands," said Grandma Lulu. "I went online using my phone, and I ordered a set of six hundred thread count Egyptian cotton sheets. If I'm living in the Northwoods of Wisconsin for the entire summer, I *must* be able to sleep better. They'll be delivered in the next day or two. Expedited shipping to the rescue!"

"Are you for real?" muttered Clare's mom.

Clare stood at the vast great room window, which overlooked the lake. She drank her juice and imagined the smell and feel of the cool water on her skin. Her legs itched to flee the cabin and leap into the glistening, graphite-colored waves.

Grandma Lulu sidled up to her. "I took the liberty of ordering *you* some new sheets, too, Clare."

"Oh, Mom. Why?" Helen groaned.

"And I ordered some for *you, too*, Helen." Grandma Lulu's grin was victorious.

"My sheets are fine. I'm used to them," said Helen.

"Me, too," said Clare.

"There's no shame in making the cabin cozier for us. As much as we loved Anthony, comfort and style were never among his priorities. Aside from that espresso maker, obviously."

At the mention of Grandpa Anthony, they all turned to the urn.

"From one mantle to another," said Clare, softly.

"But I have to admit the view here is *far* superior to that in Morrissey," said Grandma Lulu.

"When do we have to . . . you know . . . spread his

ashes?" It was such an awful question, but Clare knew she needed to address it sooner or later.

"Why don't we get settled first and decide later how we want to scatter them?" said her mom as the coffee maker growled to life.

"We've got plenty of time," said Grandma Lulu. "A whole summer's worth, in fact."

Clare nodded, thinking about her three goals. She was glad the urn would still be close by for a while. She could keep Grandpa Anthony updated on her progress.

"Speaking of getting settled, there are a bunch of things we have to accomplish today," said her mom.

The taskmaster already at work, thought Clare.

"I want you two to drive into town to pick up groceries," her mom went on. "I'll stay here to sweep and unpack. Clare, do you remember where the grocery store is, on Main Street? The bait shop, too? You can swing by and grab fishing licenses and some nightcrawlers."

"Sure," said Clare. She knew where all the stores were. The town of Alwyn was tiny, which meant that everything was located within a few blocks. Plus, she'd gone out on hundreds of errands with Grandpa Anthony.

"First, I need coffee." Grandma Lulu yawned expansively.

"Wait!" cried Clare, grabbing onto her grandmother's shoulder before she could turn away from the window. "Look!"

The feeder in the yard was suddenly swathed in little green creatures. They zipped and zinged so swiftly that Clare's eyes could hardly keep up. It was just like watching a cartoon.

Grandma Lulu stared. "They're *stunning*. I had no idea."

Clare turned to her. "Haven't you ever seen a hummingbird before?"

"Well, sure. It's just been . . . many years, I guess. I'd forgotten how enchanting they are."

"Did you know they're the smallest birds on earth? And they're the only ones that can fly backwards? They can't walk or hop since their feet are so little, but they can scoot sideways," said Clare.

"They're *marvelous*," said Grandma Lulu, taking a step closer to the window.

"I wonder what they're eating?" said Clare. "There's no way the feeder still has sugar water in it from last year."

"I bet it was the Vogels. They probably filled it when they were putting in the dock and the raft for us," said her mom.

"Bobb, Nedd, and Lloyd?" said Clare.

Her mom nodded. "They took time off from the bait shop and got the cabin all ready."

"They made the urn, too." Clare considered *that* to be the Vogel brothers' most meaningful gift to her family.

As she glanced at the urn again, she heard the faint

clink of dog tags. "Roger!" she called out. "We're in the great room. Come find us, buddy."

Clare knew he would follow the sound of her voice. She figured he'd been busy investigating the cabin, sniffing out the perimeter of every room to memorize the location of each bed, door, and sofa. He always did that in new places, presumably to avoid banging his soft, wet nose into the furniture.

"Good glory, you're covered in dust bunnies!" shrieked Grandma Lulu as Roger scampered into the room.

Clare got down on her knees to brush the fluffy balls from his brown hair. At the same time, he sneezed all over her bare legs.

"As I was saying, this place needs a good dusting," said Helen as she flung a rag at Clare.

Grandpa Anthony never cared about how clean the cabin was, or how nice the bedsheets were, thought Clare, wiping up Roger's drool. *He gave all his attention to the lake. He loved the animals and the fish, and he read good books, and he made the best campfires. That's what mattered to him.*

Grandma Lulu's cell phone buzzed.

"Gosh, Mom, it's so early for a call," said Helen.

Grandma Lulu glanced at the screen. "If you girls will excuse me." She pushed open the door to the deck and was gone in an instant.

"It must be important," said Clare. "She hasn't even poured herself a cup of coffee."

"It's probably one of her friends from Chicago, wanting to gossip."

Clare shrugged. "Well, I hope she finishes soon so we can leave. After we run our errands, I've got things to do."

"You've got *things* to do?" Her mom cackled. "You're starting to sound like *moi*, Clare Burch."

Clare began to roll her eyes, but she caught herself. Now that she had goals, maybe sounding like her mom wasn't such a bad thing, after all.

Nine
The Bait Shop

A few hours later, Grandma Lulu pulled into the parking lot of Bobb's Bait Shop. She and Clare had just finished grocery shopping.

"We got everything on your mom's list, but there weren't many options, were there? Nothing gourmet or high-end at all." Grandma Lulu pouted. "Perhaps I need to modify my expectations of Alwyn's supermarket. Or shall I call it, simply, 'market'?"

"'Market' sounds about right." Clare giggled. "But our shopping trip wasn't a failure, Grandma Lulu. We bought all those fresh cheese curds—the kind that squeak between your teeth! We found the ingredients to make my birthday cake. And we even got a tomato plant."

They swiveled to grin at the pot in the backseat. Its

soil was dark and rich, and its vibrant green stems and leaves fanned out elegantly.

"I've never been a gardener before," said Grandma Lulu. "I've never had enough patience, and I don't like getting my nails dirty."

"It helped that Grandpa Anthony always did all the yardwork," said Clare.

"True." Grandma Lulu tossed her head back and laughed. "But now I'm stepping into the wild world of tomatoes."

"There's not much we have to do to take care of the plant, Grandma Lulu. It's already in a pot. We just have to keep it in the sun and make sure it gets enough water."

"I'm glad you're feeling so confident." Grandma Lulu pulled out a tube of lipstick to apply a fresh coat. Then she turned and studied Clare's face. "You have the bluish sheen of skim milk, darling. We simply *must* get some color in you." She pinched Clare's cheeks while Clare waited. This routine had occurred more times in her life than she could count.

"Much better," said Grandma Lulu.

"Can we go in now? Please?" Clare peered through the windshield at Bobb's. From the outside, the bait shop was modest, with battered clapboard siding, cedar shingles, and a wraparound front porch. But inside, it spilled over with every kind of rod, reel, and hook an angler could want. According to Grandpa Anthony, the shop carried the biggest and best supply of bait in the North-woods.

Grandma Lulu sighed. "Yes, of course. I'm just feeling a tad nervous."

"Why would you be *nervous*? We're just buying fishing licenses!"

"I've always worried that Bobb and his brothers think I'm a snooty girl from the big city. Their best friend went off to dental school in Chicago, and he never came back. He completely changed his mind about being a dentist in Alwyn. He stayed in Morrissey with me because I didn't want to leave. The Vogels have every reason to feel resentful."

"But that's nuts. Every time I go in the shop, they ask how you are. And they drove all the way to Morrissey for Grandpa Anthony's funeral." Clare opened her car door. "I can't imagine them not liking you, but the only way to find out is to go in."

Grandma Lulu frowned.

"Are you coming or not?" said Clare.

"Yes." Grandma Lulu licked the tip of her pointer finger and smoothed her eyebrows. "I'm coming."

Bells jingled merrily on the door of the bait shop, announcing their arrival. "Here we are!" said Clare. "It's not so bad, is it?"

Grandma Lulu removed her sunglasses.

"There are so many cool things," continued Clare.

"Come on, I'll show you around." She pulled her grandmother down an aisle, which was as colorful and eye-catching as any fancy shop back in Chicago. She pointed out the tackle that Grandpa Anthony had always bought for her: bobbers, sinkers, stringers, topwater baits, and fishhooks.

Grandma Lulu examined each of the items. "I have no clue what any of these things are, but they remind me of the charms I have on my necklaces and bracelets. They're like little pieces of jewelry."

Clare nodded. She loved that fishing tackle wasn't just practical; it was pretty, too.

An aisle over, a few people were arguing enthusiastically about which house in town needed to be repainted and who had made the best tuna noodle casserole for the latest church potluck. As Clare eavesdropped, she was reminded of how different Alwyn and Morrissey were from each other. "I can't believe we're in the same time zone as Chicago," she whispered to her grandmother.

But Grandma Lulu was still looking at the intricate swivels and hooks of the fishing lures. "You actually *catch fish* with these?"

Clare nodded.

"How on earth do you know which ones to use?"

"Grandpa Anthony taught me. It depends on what species you're after. Like, if you're fishing for walleye, you use jigs." Clare showed Grandma Lulu the jigs, which were small lead ball-and-hooks that came in every shade of the rainbow. "You spear nightcrawlers right onto the jigs—and you can even buy the nightcrawlers here. They're in containers in the refrigerator over there. Leeches, too, if you like those better."

"Leeches?" Grandma Lulu looked aghast. "Do you *touch* them?"

Clare was about ready to say, *"Yes, I touch them,"* but the storage room door swung open, and Bobb Vogel marched in. He reminded Clare of a parade marshal, minus the white gloves and baton.

"Is that *Clare Burch*?" Bobb's smile was wide as a platter. "Get over here and give this old man a hug!"

Clare scurried into Bobb's arms, and he gave her the kind of engulfing embrace she hadn't had since her grandfather died.

Grandma Lulu stepped toward them, a blush creeping up into her neck. "Why hello, Bobb."

"Gol-darn, it's good to see you, Louise! And this time, mercifully, not at a funeral." Bobb leaned in to kiss her cheeks: right, left, right again. "The Burch girls up north together! Anthony would be pleased as punch."

Between his bristly hair, bristly mustache, and bristly voice, Bobb Vogel reminded Clare of a nub of frayed rope.

"It's nice to be here." Grandma Lulu fluffed her hair and smiled bashfully.

Clare wondered if aliens had abducted her grand-mother.

"So, we need to get fishing licenses," she said to Bobb. "My mom put it on our to-do list for the day. If we come back without them, she might seriously ground us."

"Fishing licenses, you betcha." Bobb pointed his finger in the air. "We don't want you to get grounded." He went behind the counter and pulled out a small machine that looked like a receipt-printer. He began to punch in information. "How many would you ladies like? Clare, you don't need one, right? Since you're still under sixteen?"

"Correct," said Clare. "But tomorrow's my birthday. I'll be thirteen." *A teenager! It sounds so old!*

"Well, happy early birthday, sweetheart. June third, hey? Did ya know you were born on the feast day of Saint Kevin?"

The only thing Clare knew about St. Kevin was that their church in Morrissey was named after him.

"Patron saint of blackbirds. Lover of otters. Happiest when hanging out with the animals in the valley of the two lakes in Ireland," said Bobb. "Legend says that a crow laid an egg in Saint Kevin's hand while his arms were out-stretched in prayer. He didn't move until the baby bird hatched. Crazy, eh?"

Clare's eyes widened. She loved that he knew all that, right off the top of his head. Her grandmother was staring at Bobb, too.

"Anywho," he continued, "I know you'll want a fishing license for Helen. And what about you, Louise? Do you need a fishing license, too?"

"Why, yes, thank you," said Grandma Lulu.

"*You're* getting a fishing license?" said Clare.

"Yes, darling, but there's no need to make a big deal out of it."

"But why?"

"To fish, of course."

Now Clare was staring at her grandmother.

Grandma Lulu shrugged. "You know the expression, 'When in Rome . . .'"

"Will you be able to pick up a nightcrawler with your bare hand? Will you freak out if you actually catch a fish?" said Clare.

"Hey there, go easy on your grandma," said Bobb, with a wink. "She just wants to make the most of her time up north."

"Thank you, Bobb," said Grandma Lulu, with a prim smile.

Clare tried to wipe the look of shock off her face.

Bobb gazed over the counter at her. "So, Clare, you wanna try for a musky this summer, or no?"

"Yes," she replied. "I *do* want to try for a musky this summer, but I don't know how to fish for them. Grandpa Anthony was going to teach me."

"Well, it's a cryin' shame you don't know anybody else

who happens to be a musky expert in these parts," said Bobb, with a straight face.

Clare started to laugh.

"My brothers and I would be glad to teach you."

"Thanks. I'd love that." She was one step closer to goal number three!

Bobb nodded, and his little machine spat out two rectangles of paper. He handed Clare the fishing licenses. "You're all set."

Grandma Lulu cleared her voice. "Before we leave, Bobb, I wanted to thank you, Nedd, and Lloyd for filling up our hummingbird feeder—and for putting in the dock and the raft. I can only imagine how much work that was."

"Always glad to lend a hand, Louise."

"And thank you for making the urn, too," said Clare. "It's really beautiful. Grandpa Anthony's in it right now. On the mantle, actually."

"Well, goodness. Anthony was like a brother to us. It was an honor to make that urn for him. I felt pretty awful about his passing, but when the universe asks you to do something difficult, you gotta listen up and do it." Bobb dipped his head and swiped a calloused hand across his eyes.

At the same time, heavy footfalls clumped on the shop's porch.

The front door jangled open, and two Bobb-lookalikes tramped in. Nedd and Lloyd shared the same stubbly cheeks, bright blue eyes, and tufts of gray-and-white hair as their older brother. Clare thought they belonged on the front cover of a Wisconsin outdoor magazine. They were wearing fishing vests and hats, polarized sunglasses, and water sandals. They carried a jumble of fishing rods, tackle boxes, and insulated lunch sacks that she assumed were stuffed with cold drinks and containers of live bait. A whiff of sunscreen and perspiration lingered in their wake.

Clare opened her mouth to greet them, but nothing passed her lips. The Vogels were walking, talking, very living reminders of her grandfather. *Why do Nedd and Lloyd get to spend a perfect June morning fishing on the lake, but Grandpa Anthony doesn't get to do anything because he's dead?*

She felt the familiar pinch of blame and regret.

If I were faster and had gotten to him sooner, maybe he'd still be alive.

"Aw geez, look who's here!" yelled Nedd, slicing right through Clare's dismay. He and Lloyd dumped their gear behind the register and opened their arms to Clare and Grandma Lulu. As they hugged, Nedd and Lloyd began asking a barrage of questions in their bottomless, booming voices. Clare loved their funny expressions and spacious Wisconsin vowels, and she wondered if Grandpa Anthony had ever talked like that when he was young and still living in Alwyn.

"How does it feel to be done with seventh grade, Kitty-

Clare?" said Lloyd, patting her back. His hand was as large as a bear paw.

"I'm glad it's over," said Clare.

"I can't imagine it was easy," said Nedd.

You have no idea, thought Clare.

"And you, Louise? Chicago's still treating you well?" said Lloyd.

"Oh, yes," said Grandma Lulu.

"How was it out on the water, boys?" said Bobb.

"Fair to midlin'," said Lloyd, fanning his face with his fishing hat.

"Caught a couple-two-three," said Nedd.

"All yellow perch," said Lloyd. "I'll fry 'em up for supper tonight."

"What are they biting on these days?" asked Clare.

"We've been using leeches, but we'll switch things up soon," said Lloyd. "Gotta keep 'em guessing."

"Good glory," said Grandma Lulu under her breath. "Leeches."

"And how's Helen?" said Nedd.

"She's keeping Clare and me in line," said Grandma Lulu.

"As always," said Clare, rolling her eyes.

"And the cabin? Is everything all right for you ladies?" said Bobb.

"Oh, yes," said Clare. "It's great, and I can't wait to swim out to the raft. Thanks for putting it in for us."

"The lake thawed a little early this year," said Nedd. "Gave us plenty of time to get things ready for you girls."

"The hummingbird food was a perfect touch," said Grandma Lulu.

Thank goodness she didn't say anything about the bedsheets! thought Clare.

"Hey, what about that humdinger of a musky rod you've got, Kitty-Clare? Is it ready for some action this summer?" said Lloyd.

"Yes, but I'll need help. I have no idea what I'm doing."

"Okie dokie," said Nedd, bowing. "At your service."

"Me too," said Lloyd, smooshing his hat back on his head.

"One more thing before you go." Bobb dug around behind the register and handed Clare a bulging paper bag.

She took the bag from him and peered inside. It was filled with her favorite candy, and it smelled like a sugar-bomb had just gone off. She decided that if Grandpa Anthony couldn't be there to buy her Caramel Dots, Bobb Vogel was the next best option.

"Just make sure you brush your teeth after you eat them. I don't wanna be responsible for any cavities, OK?" he whispered.

"OK." Clare felt her eyes get drippy. "Thanks, Bobb."

Bobb reached across the register and squeezed her shoulder. "Aw, don't mention it."

"All right, darling," said Grandma Lulu, clapping her

hands. "It's time to go. We need to head home so we can put our groceries away and bake your birthday cake."

Did my grandmother just use the word 'home'? Like it was no big deal? wondered Clare. *Maybe she's already starting to feel like she belongs here, after all!*

The Vogel brothers called out their birthday wishes as Clare pushed the door open. She and Grandma Lulu waved goodbye while the bells clanged overhead.

"How do you think it went?" said Clare when they got to the car.

"Honestly, darling, those Vogel boys are lovely."

"Told ya so," she replied, sounding very Wisconsin.

Grandma Lulu poked her head in the backseat and shrieked at their slightly wilting tomato plant. "Is it going to die?" she cried.

"I don't think so," said Clare, gently petting one of its leaves. "It'll be OK. We just need to get it . . . home."

Ten
Thirteen

Clare kicked off her birthday with an early-morning swim. Finally, she could get in the lake! She felt her
mother's eyes on her as she tore down the dock.

"Don't run, Clare! For heaven's sake, I don't want you
to trip or get hurt!" Helen called from the great room
window.

Clare smiled underneath her goggles and swim cap.
No diving here, she reminded herself as she leaped into
the water. It was too shallow along the shoreline. She
needed to wait until the raft, where it was deep and safe.

The water was as pure and bracing as she anticipat-
ed. She got shivers up and down her arms and legs, but
she knew the temperature of the lake would warm up as
summer went on.

Clare pointed her fingers. Her limbs and lungs knew

what to do as she launched into a front crawl. Left arm, right arm, breathing every few strokes, all while kicking, kicking, kicking, steadily churning the water behind her. She did thirteen laps, in honor of her brand-new age. When she ended up at the raft, she climbed the ladder and waved at her mother, who was still watching.

"I'm fine!" she shouted.

Her mom blew her a kiss.

Clare sat on the raft and gazed into the unending blue above her. Unlike Chicago, Alwyn wasn't smoggy or gray.

"I'm thirteen today," she said to the sky.

Her announcement was met by the cawing of crows. She removed her goggles and counted them—thirteen altogether—gliding in broad arcs above her. They called out noisily to each other, and Clare wondered what information they were swapping. She remembered from her school project that crows had the biggest brain-to-body ratio of all bird species. They could sing a bunch of different melodies and even imitate human voices, operas, and the ringing of cell phones.

Crows are some of the most intelligent creatures on earth, she thought. *I get why Saint Kevin liked them so much.*

After a few minutes of watching them swoop and soar, Clare was ready to swim again. *Thirteen more laps, because why not?*

Then she would need to take a shower and get dressed for her first day as a teenager.

"I gotta go now," she called out to the crows. Her mom and Grandma Lulu were taking her into town for a birthday lunch at Dutch's, her favorite restaurant in Alwyn. She couldn't wait to sink her teeth into some crunchy, greasy onion rings and a grilled cheese sandwich. Then they were going to her first-ever water ski show. And *then* they were going to eat cake—lots of cake. Red velvet with buttercream frosting, which they had baked the day before. She hoped all these things would help her forget about the fact that she couldn't celebrate with Olive and Emmy.

Clare affixed her goggles and stood up. She rolled her shoulders and flapped her arms back and forth to get the blood moving through them again. She curled the toes of her left foot over the edge of the raft, with her right foot behind. She crouched and tucked her head. Then she stretched her arms forward to grab the raft with her fingers.

"It's not a starting block, but it'll have to work," she said.

She closed her eyes like she'd learned from her coaches, removing her sense of sight so her sense of hearing would be heightened. She pretended that Olive was on one side of her, and Emmy on the other. She knew they were practicing in Morrissey at that same moment.

"Take your mark," she intoned, just like the starter at a swim meet. She imitated the buzzer—a short, sharp drone—and her muscles sprang to action.

Pushing off the raft using her hands, feet and toes, Clare exploded upward and outward. She locked her elbows by her ears and pointed her toes. As she blasted under the surface of the lake, the boom of white noise filled her ears, and she felt a cold effervescence rise from somewhere below her. She transitioned into the butterfly, throwing her arms up and out of the water while doing a dolphin kick. She progressed like a graceful wave toward shore.

When Clare's toes began to touch the rocky bottom of the lake by the Burches' dock, she slowed her stroke and took in great gulps of air, thanking her body for remembering what to do.

"Get ready, Lake Alwyn," she said to the bubbling water as she waded out. "I'll be doing that swim on repeat this summer."

She grabbed her beach towel from the damp grass.

"Goal number two, here I come."

Eleven
The Fishbowl

Later that afternoon, Clare and her mom found a row of open seats on the crowded bleachers that lined one of the bays of Lake Lyons.

"I automatically like any place that's called the Fishbowl," said Clare.

The Fishbowl was packed with tourists, summer residents, and Northwoods locals alike. They were all assembled to watch the first Al-Skis show of the season, and they were buzzing with so much laughter and conversation that Clare felt like she was sitting in a beehive.

"Why haven't we come here before? It's really cool."

"I guess it wasn't your grandfather's thing," said her mom.

"I wonder if it could become *our* thing?" Clare liked the idea of her family coming up with their own new traditions.

"Sure," said her mom. "Why not? It's our chance to start over in some ways."

Two teenagers welcomed the audience using cordless microphones. They wore white shorts and navy-blue Al-Ski t-shirts, and Clare thought they looked impossibly tan for the first week of June.

"My name is Lucy," said the girl announcer. "On behalf of the Al-Skis Water Ski Club, welcome to our new season!"

"My name is Jeffrey," said the boy announcer. "The Al-Skis originated fifty years ago, and we remain the oldest amateur water ski show in the country. Each summer we hold auditions, and we perform three times a week."

"Don't forget to visit our snack shack!" Lucy gestured to the concessions stand in the parking lot. "We've got lots of great treats."

Clare craned her neck to look at her grandmother, who was chatting with two women in front of the snack shack. "Who is Grandma Lulu talking to?"

"I don't know," said her mom. "I can't keep up with her."

"Our skiers aren't just talented," continued Jeffrey, "they're brave, too, because our boats go as fast as forty-five miles per hour."

Clare wrinkled her nose. "I can't imagine doing that. I'll just stick with swimming and fishing."

"That's a lot more than most people do," said her mom.

"I guess," said Clare.

"We've got some great new moves to show you today," said Lucy, "so let's start the show!"

The crowd began to chant, "Al-Skis! Al-Skis! Al-Skis!" Clare and her mom joined in.

Clare watched the skiers emerge from a boathouse next to the bleachers. The girls sported tight buns on their heads, sequined outfits, and flashy makeup that she knew Grandma Lulu would adore. The boys wore sparkly swim trunks and had slicked-back hair. Even though Clare preferred the simple, stripped-down uniform of swim team, she found herself wondering what it would be like to participate in a show like that.

While the skiers waited to perform, they goofed around and tossed candy into the audience, sending kids scrambling to claim the pieces. Clare's mom got pegged in the leg with a jumbo Fudgie Chew. She picked it up and handed it to Clare. "For you."

"Share it?" Clare bit off half and handed the rest to her mother, who stuffed it in her mouth. They giggled as they tried to swallow the gooey mess.

If it were a regular summer night back in Morrissey, what would I be doing right now? wondered Clare. She figured she'd be with Olive and Emmy, or reading a book, or walking Roger. She knew for sure she wouldn't be hanging out with her mom.

Maybe being in Alwyn for the summer had some benefits.

Some of the water-skiers did tricks solo. They swiveled, jumped, and flipped while never losing their grip on the tow rope. Some were part of a duo or trio. They skied barefoot or balanced in headstands on top of saucers. Others linked arms and stacked themselves in three, or four, or even five rows to create towering human pyramids. The top point of the pyramid was one of the smallest and most nimble skiers, waving an Al-Skis flag from twenty-five feet above the water.

Clare wondered what it took to do a trick like that in front of everyone. She imagined how free and agile the girl on top of the pyramid must feel, soaring above the lake and bleachers like a bird. She snapped a picture and texted it to Olive and Emmy. *Crazy,* she typed.

Emmy responded right away. *You should totally do that!*

No way. I don't even know how to water-ski.

So learn, Olive texted back.

Clare rolled her eyes. *LOL. Whatever.*

At intermission, Clare told her mom how much she'd loved the first part of the show. "But Grandma Lulu is missing everything. Why isn't she sitting here with us?"

"She's too busy socializing, I guess." Clare's mom smiled. "Unlike me, she's got a flair for making friends wherever she goes."

"Let's go see what's up." Clare climbed off the bleachers with Helen behind her. As she headed toward the snack shack, she passed by clumps of teenagers who were talking and shrieking with laughter. She tried to hold her head high.

I have friends, too! she wanted to tell them. *They're just . . . far away.*

Twelve
Not One but Two

The snack shack was mobbed, but Grandma Lulu materialized from the throng of hungry people. She walked toward Clare and her mom holding two snow cones aloft. "I beat the crowd, darlings!"

"It's because you've been standing here the whole time, Mom," said Helen, dryly.

"I got cherry for you, Helen. And grape for you, Clare. Now, please don't be cross with me. I know I've missed half the show, but I've met some delightful people that I'm so excited to introduce you to." Grandma Lulu placed her arms around the shoulders of the two women. "This is Abby and Marisa Porter. Abby and Marisa, meet my daughter, Helen, and my granddaughter, Clare."

"I feel like I already know you guys after hearing Louise gush about you," said Abby. She was tall, trim, blond, and very muscular. When she shook Clare's hand, Clare briefly wondered if her finger bones had broken in half.

"I'm so glad Lola and Theo will have a new friend this summer," said Marisa. She looked like Abby's polar opposite; she was petite, and her dark curly hair was raked into a floppy ponytail. "But I guess I'm getting ahead of myself. Sorry, no pressure or anything!"

Are you kidding? Clare thought about goal number one and smiled back at Marisa.

"Speaking of Lola and Theo . . ." Marisa pulled two kids to her side. "Here they are!"

Clare hadn't realized they all belonged together; they looked so different from one another. Despite her sweet, purple snow cone, her mouth grew dry. It had been so long since she'd met someone new. What if she didn't know what to say? What if they didn't like her?

"Lola's a year younger than you, Clare," said Marisa. "She'll be in seventh grade. Theo is ten, and he'll be in fifth grade."

"Hi," said Lola.

"Hi," said Theo.

But before Clare could say hi back, Marisa went on. "We've lived in Alwyn since last August. We moved here from Milwaukee so Abby could open her boxing gym on Main Street. And if you're wondering why in the world she decided to open a boxing gym in the Northwoods—well, it's because our family wanted a change. Sometimes you just have to get rid of everything that feels familiar to see the world in a new way! And Abby says that people who fish need to build their upper-body strength—and what better way to work your shoulders, biceps, and triceps than boxing?"

"Swimming?" Clare managed to say.

"Yes!" Abby grinned. "Swimming!"

"I'm a business consultant, which means I work on my laptop all day instead of hitting a punching bag, so unfortunately my muscles look *nothing* like Abby's," continued Marisa.

Clare wondered how she managed to talk for so long without taking a breath.

"And, in case you're curious, because it always comes up sooner or later, we adopted Lola from South Korea and Theo from Ethiopia. Abby's family is Scandinavian, and mine is from Brazil, so I guess you could say we're like a mini United Nations." Marisa smiled radiantly.

Lola and Theo rolled their eyes at each other, which made Clare giggle behind her snow cone.

Abby turned to Marisa with a pained expression.

"Oh, gosh . . . I'm so sorry," said Marisa. "I'm doing all the talking for everyone, aren't I? Abby says I like to chat too much. I'm trying to work on it, I swear!"

Abby snorted and patted Marisa's shoulder. "So, I understand we're practically neighbors with you guys," she said to Clare. "Even though our cottage is on Lake Lyons, we're just on the other side of that tiny strip of land that runs between Lake Lyons and Lake Alwyn."

"The isthmus?" said Clare.

Abby nodded.

"Could you please define 'isthmus'?" said Theo. He looked up at Clare through his thick tortoiseshell eyeglasses. He seemed like the kids in Clare's class that always sat in the front row and raised their hands whenever they got the chance. But she didn't find him annoying at all. Instead, she wanted to pat him on the head and give him a sticker.

"It's a thin strip of land that runs between two bodies of water. Our isthmus is pretty narrow—just six feet across. It's wet and grassy, with a few trees growing on it. There's a big pipe that runs through it, too, called a culvert. It means that water is always flowing from Lake Lyons into Lake Alwyn," said Clare.

"The two lakes are attached?" asked Lola.

Clare noticed that they were about the same height. She also noticed Lola's enviable black braid snaking down her back.

"Yep, I'll show you sometime. You can even portage between them. My grandpa and mom and I used to paddle our canoe over to the isthmus when we wanted a change from Lake Alwyn. We'd climb out and drag the canoe across. Then we'd push it into Lake Lyons so we could have a different place to fish."

"Did you ever catch anything?" said Abby.

"Totally," said Clare. She smiled at her mom as she thought of the hours they'd spent hauling in walleyes and northern pike with Grandpa Anthony. "Some days are slower than others, but there are always fish out there, somewhere."

"Would you guys mind if I asked for advice sometime?" said Abby. "I've tried to teach myself how to fish, but I haven't been very successful."

"Sure," said Helen. "Do you have the right equipment? Have you been to Bobb's Bait Shop to check out the nightcrawlers and leeches?"

Oh my gosh, is she actually trying to make a friend? wondered Clare. *Come on, Mom, you can do it!*

Within seconds, Helen was deep in conversation with Abby and Marisa.

Clare couldn't remember the last time she'd watched her mother interact with someone her own age, let alone *two* people. Clare saw how cheerful she looked, her red hair glinting in the late-afternoon rays of sun. Abby and Marisa were asking about her job as an art teacher at the high school in Morrissey, and her mom was telling them about her love of painting.

Clare felt a tap on her shoulder.

"I want to come to every single Al-Skis performance this year," said Theo. "This is my first one, and I am very impressed."

"Me too," said Clare. "That's a lot of shows, though." She counted in her head. "Like thirty-six or something."

"Well, I don't know what else we'll be doing." Theo shrugged. "It's our first summer here, so it's all new to me."

"I bet we can figure out some things to do. I've got a raft and a canoe and a fishing boat—and also a super cute dog who loves getting attention." Clare's mouth didn't feel dry anymore. She let the ice particles from her snow cone dissolve on her tongue, and she smiled a numb, grape smile.

"That sounds awesome," said Theo.

"Sorry," Lola whispered to Clare. "It's so annoying having a little brother following me around all the time."

"I always thought it'd be fun to have a brother or sister," said Clare.

"Not really. You can borrow him for the summer." Lola flipped her braid like a jump rope, and she grinned.

Clare giggled.

"He's not so bad to have around, actually," said Lola, nudging Theo.

"Ow," said Theo. He nudged her back.

"So, your grandma said you've come up to Alwyn for a week every summer since you were little," said Lola. "It'll be nice having you around."

"Thanks. I'm glad you're here, too. I've never had any friends up north. I've always just hung out with my mom and Grandpa Anthony, but now that he's gone, I guess I need to branch out a little bit."

"I'm sorry about your grandfather," said Lola.

"Me too," said Theo.

"Me three," said Clare, but as she said the words, she realized that her eyes hadn't welled up, and it no longer felt like her insides were lined with barbed wire. This seemed like an encouraging sign.

Just then, Helen's voice rang out. Clare couldn't remember the last time it had sounded so jovial. "Clare! How would you feel about having the Porters over for cake and ice cream after the show?"

Clare looked at Lola and Theo. They nodded their heads vigorously.

"Is it your birthday?" said Lola. "We love cake."

Clare nodded shyly. "I'm thirteen."

"Happy birthday!" said Theo. "We love ice cream, too."

Clare thought of the goal she'd set for herself: make a new friend in Alwyn. She pictured the huge red velvet cake waiting for them at the cabin—and Roger, who would pant in delight at meeting the Porters.

"That sounds great, Mom," she said.

Looking extremely pleased with herself, Grandma Lulu nudged Clare in the direction of the Fishbowl. "Then why don't you kids go watch the rest of the show while the moms talk? We'll meet you right here when it's over."

Clare, Lola, and Theo started to walk toward the bleachers. As they fell in step with each other, a boy on a bike intercepted their path.

"Ugh," said Theo.

"It's Jack," said Lola.

The boy circled them a few times and then stopped directly in front of Clare. She couldn't move forward. She looked down at her sneakers, wondering what to do.

"Hey," said Jack, "who's *this*?"

Clare could feel him peering at her.

"Oh, leave her alone," said Theo.

"This is Clare. She's from Chicago, and she's very nice. Now move along, please," said Lola, flapping her hand.

Clare didn't know if she should say hi or push the bike aside or walk clear around it.

"Chicago? Ooh, a city girl."

The sprawling way Jack pronounced "Chicaaagooo" reminded Clare of the Vogel brothers.

"At least she's from America, unlike you two, who are from Mozambique or Zimbabwe or wherever," said Jack.

"That would be South Korea for Lola, and Ethiopia for me," said Theo, pushing his glasses up the bridge of his nose. "But I'm impressed you at least got one of the continents correct."

"Africa." Lola clapped her hands sarcastically. "Bravo."

"Whatever," said Jack.

Clare wondered if he ever got tired of looking so peevish all the time.

"Are we gonna have some fun together this summer,

or no?" said Jack. He raked his hand through his mop of overgrown brown hair.

"Definitely not," said Lola under her breath.

At the same time, a man—Clare assumed it was his dad—yelled from the parking lot. "Yo! Jackson!"

Cringing, Jack rode off, disappearing into the swarm of people.

"What's his deal?" asked Clare.

"He's a jerk," said Lola. "He goes to our school. He'll be in seventh grade, like me."

"Oh," said Clare. She had never thought about the possibility of there being jerks in Alwyn. She'd assumed that everyone up north was nice.

As they settled on the bleachers to watch the second half of the Al-Skis show, Clare kept picturing Jack's face. She didn't want to see it again anytime soon.

But then Lola placed two fingertips in her mouth and began to whistle at the skiers.

Theo covered his ears and laughed.

Lola's whistling, which sounded just like a screaming firecracker, was so loud that Clare almost didn't hear the new little voice coming from inside her head.

You've got two new friends, and you're thirteen now, it said.

Clare plugged her ears like Theo. She listened more closely.

You can handle anything—even a jerk in Alwyn.

Thirteen
The Fiddlehead Fern

Another early-morning swim.

Without fail, Clare was sticking to the daily training regimen she'd set for herself. Back and forth, between the dock and the raft, she did the butterfly, breaststroke, and front crawl, feeling oxygen surge through her body in a thrilling *whoosh*. With each lap, she imagined that she was growing as strong as Abby. With each lap, she was one step closer to achieving her goal of swimming out to the island and back.

In an hour or less.

Without wearing a life jacket.

She imagined Grandpa Anthony waving his arms and hollering, just like he'd always done at her swim meets. "Don't stop, Clare! Push a little harder! Leave it all in the water!"

She would forever miss his cheering, but she knew that any progress she made now was hers alone.

Through her goggles, Clare could see the island way out in the middle of the lake, like a gigantic, unmoving turtle. Right then, she decided she would do her big swim in August, before going back to Morrissey for eighth grade. She needed as much time as possible to prepare.

Clare approached the raft. Without looking—because she'd figured out exactly where she needed to be in order to begin her flip turn—she pulled her knees and chin into her chest and propelled herself into a half-somersault. Pushing off the side of the raft with her legs, she pointed back toward shore.

As she swam to the dock, Clare thought about how comfortable she was starting to feel in Alwyn, and how quickly it was happening, and all the things she was discovering about herself along the way.

She'd learned that she loved to spy on hummingbirds as they hovered around the feeder, tadpoles as they wriggled through the lake, and bald eagles as they built their nests in the highest treetops. She noticed all the plants and flowers, too, which were sprouting up every place she looked, even in cracks in the sidewalk. Grandpa Anthony had pointed out all the vegetation to her when she was a little kid, and she was glad she hadn't forgotten: *starflower, wild calla, wood sorrel, goldthread*. When she said their names, they felt like a mash-up of poetry and science in her mouth.

Clare reached the dock. It was too shallow for her to flip, so she simply stood up and turned around. *It's not as smooth as doing laps in the pool, but I'll get used to it,* she thought. *At least I'm out here training and staying in shape.*

Swimming had always been something she'd had to work hard at. Some kids on her team were naturally sleek and fast and broke all the pool records, but Clare had never been like that. Most of the time, she was somewhere in the middle. She wished she were quicker, but she knew that getting in the water every day was the most important thing.

As Clare kicked, feeling bubbles bounce off her fingers and toes, she thought about Lola and Theo. She couldn't believe they'd hung out every single day since they'd met at the Al-Skis show.

I still miss you guys, but I made two new friends, Clare had texted to Olive and Emmy.

SO glad you're putting yourself out there!!! Emmy wrote back.

They sound amazing, texted Olive. *But not as amazing as yours truly. Ha.*

Clare finished up her final lap of the morning. She waded out of the lake and walked up the sloping lawn, running her hand across a swishy patch of fiddlehead ferns. She loved to watch their tips loosen and carefully release their tightly coiled shoots of new life.

They're sort of like me, she thought. *I'm changing into something that was there all along, I just didn't know it.*

Voices from the cabin interrupted Clare's thoughts. It sounded like her mom, Grandma Lulu, and someone else she didn't know. She watched in confusion as a woman pushed open the door and walked outside. *I didn't even realize anybody was here.*

The woman was wearing an uncomfortable-looking pencil skirt and blazer, and she carried a camera and an armful of folders. Her hairdo was so stiff that Clare wondered if it would suffice as a bike helmet. Helen and Grandma Lulu waved goodbye as the woman climbed into her car and drove away.

"Who was that?" asked Clare when she got inside.

Her mom frowned, and Grandma Lulu tugged at one of her curls. *Boing.*

Clare noticed that neither of them would meet her eye. "What's going on?"

"Oh, darling," said Grandma Lulu.

"It's complicated," said her mom.

"*What's* complicated? *Nothing* is supposed to be complicated now that we're finally in Alwyn for the summer," said Clare. "I had enough *complications* back in Morrissey, ever since Grandpa Anthony died!" She could feel the lake water trickling from her suit and pooling under her bare, grass-stained feet. She wrapped her beach towel tighter around her body, as if it were a suit of armor.

Her mom sighed. "The woman who was just here is a realtor. Her name is Juliet."

"A realtor? Why?" Even under her thick beach towel, Clare felt her skin prickle into cold little bumps.

"In his will, Grandpa Anthony left the cabin to Grandma Lulu," said her mom. "And now, Grandma Lulu is planning to sell it."

"Sell the cabin?" Clare could barely form the words.

"Without Anthony, I just don't think it's wise to hang on to it," said Grandma Lulu. "It's expensive, and it requires a lot of upkeep, and we'll never, ever use it as much as he did. You know he was always sneaking up here whenever he could get away, but I don't foresee us doing that." She held her palms up, as if asking Clare for forgiveness.

"But . . ." Clare shook her head frantically. "I thought we were having a great summer? I thought you were *enjoying* being up north? I thought we'd gotten into a nice *routine*? I thought you bought sheets for the beds so that we'd all be *comfortable*?"

"Yes, to all those things!" said Grandma Lulu. "I'm having a delightful time. I've fallen in love with shopping at the market and grilling our dinner on the deck and watering our tomato plant and taking Roger on walks through the woods—but that's not the issue."

"Then what *is* the issue?"

"What happens when we go back to Morrissey?" said her mom. "It's takes a lot of time to care for the cabin—

and the dock, raft, canoe, and fishing boat. Your grandpa always used to handle those things. I love this cabin as much as you do, but it's just not prudent for us to keep it. I wish it were a different story."

"Prudent." Clare couldn't remember what *prudent* meant. Her mind had gone dark. She groped around for a light switch.

"I know this is very upsetting, darling, but we'll enjoy every minute of our summer, and we'll go out with a bang," said Grandma Lulu. "Before we leave, we'll scatter your grandfather's ashes just like he wanted, and then Juliet will put the cabin on the market for us."

Clare's fingertips were turning blue. She was shivering and needed to take a hot shower. "So I guess it's a done deal, then?" She spat out the words. Before her mom or grandmother could answer, she stormed out of the kitchen.

Slamming the bathroom door behind her, Clare imagined the tip of a fiddlehead fern rolling back up and curling in on itself.

Fourteen
It's Not Fish They're After

After her shower—which, unfortunately, did not wash away the memory of Juliet's face or the ridiculousness of Grandma Lulu's plan to sell the cabin—Clare locked herself in her bedroom with Roger. She curled up like a donut, placing him in the middle. Her very own donut hole.

She sniffled into his velvety ears and began to breathe more slowly.

Life is hard and confusing and messy, she thought. *But I don't want to spend the whole afternoon in bed. I've felt sorry for myself too much this year, and it's never been worth it.*

"Maybe Lola and Theo would want to go fishing with me?" she said into Roger's fur.

His tail beat against her leg.

Clare laughed and rubbed his head. "Thanks, pup. I'm glad you approve."

And within an hour, Clare was in the canoe with her friends.

She, Lola, and Theo drifted lazily across Lake Alwyn, hoping to catch a walleye or smallmouth bass. Clare was using a lure that Grandma Lulu had bought for her at Bobb's because the glittery rubber had reminded her of a disco ball.

Clare cast her line.

Lola and Theo cast theirs.

"I can't believe your grandma wants to sell the cabin!" wailed Theo.

"I don't think she *wants* to. It's just that my grandpa dying has changed a lot of things," said Clare.

Lola sighed. "Maybe we could visit you in Chicago."

"And you could come to Alwyn and stay with us sometime," said Theo.

"I'd love that." Clare's voice faded as they cast their lines again.

"You have so much patience," said Lola, a few minutes later.

"What do you mean?" said Clare.

"I start to go stir crazy when I've been sitting in a boat for so long."

"Then maybe you should just stick with your talent of being in Drama Club, Lola," said Theo. "You're *very* good at being theatrical."

"Why, thank you, little brother," said Lola, in a perfect British accent.

"I bet you're amazing on stage," said Clare, imagining Lola in costume under the bright lights. Lola's bravado seemed much more exciting than her own quiet watchfulness.

"Why do you like fishing so much, anyway?" asked Lola.

Clare thought for a moment. "My grandpa started taking me fishing as soon as I could hold a rod. He taught me that you have to be patient and calm when you're out on the water, but you also have to be constantly thinking and assessing."

"So, basically, you're saying that fishing is relaxing and *not* relaxing at the same time?" Lola smacked her forehead. "Good grief."

"Do you think there are any fish out there right now?" asked Theo. "Because I'd really like to catch one."

"Sure," said Clare, "but we're trying to fool them on their own turf. We've got to find the right combination of things, like the bait we're using and the way we cast, to get their attention. They've got all their senses, and they aren't easily tricked."

"So in the meantime, we just relax," said Lola, "and *not* relax."

Theo cleared his throat. "To quote Henry David Thoreau, 'Many men go fishing all their lives without knowing that it is not fish they are after.'"

"Theo!" said Lola.

"Sorry," he said. "'Many *women* and men go fishing all of their lives without knowing that it is not fish they are after.'"

"Thank you," said Lola. "We're an equal opportunity boat."

"How do you know that line, Theo?" asked Clare. She loved it when anyone quoted a line from a book or poem from memory.

"We talked about Thoreau in school," said Theo. "He wrote *Walden*. It's about living simply in natural surroundings. On a pond, actually. In Massachusetts."

Clare considered Thoreau's line. She definitely wanted a musky, but she wondered if there was something more that she was after. *I guess I'll have to figure that out,* she thought.

"Do you feel like when you finally catch a fish, it was meant to be?" asked Theo.

"Sort of," said Clare. "It's a combination of skill, patience, strength, and being prepared, all mixed together with an element of good luck. You do everything in your control to be ready, but then you have to let go of any expectations, because either you'll catch something—"

"Or you won't," said Lola.

Suddenly, Theo screeched. "I'm getting a bite!" The end of his pole dipped toward the water.

"Pull back and set the hook!" yelled Clare.

But as soon as Theo started to reel, the fish shook free. "Darn."

"Sorry, Theo. It happens to me all the time."

"I'm jealous you almost had one. That's way more than I've gotten today," said Lola.

By now, the canoe had bobbed all the way over to the isthmus. Clare remembered how she and her mom and Grandpa Anthony had portaged across the grassy, narrow strip of land. She'd loved to stand in the very center of the isthmus, with Lake Alwyn on one side and Lake Lyons on the other. To her, it was twice the view—and the beauty.

The culvert connecting the lakes bubbled and frothed.

As Clare was ready to fire another cast, a blur of movement caught her eye. A few little heads poked out of the culvert. "You guys! Look!" She pointed. Three dark brown creatures shimmied out of the pipe and slithered onto the isthmus.

"Oh, my gosh, what *are* they?" said Lola.

"They're river otters, Lo. I think it's a mama and two babies."

"They're adorable," said Theo.

They watched the otters slink and tumble. Their wet bodies moved with circus-like flexibility.

"They're playing with each other!" said Lola.

"It looks like they're wrestling. One of them keeps bothering the other. They won't leave each other alone," said Theo.

"Just like how *you* won't leave *me* alone," said Lola.

Theo stuck his tongue out at her.

But the otters had stopped playing. They'd turned their heads toward Lake Lyons, their bodies unmoving. Tree branches snapped and the tall grass was pushed aside as a person emerged, dragging a dinghy onto the land.

"No way," said Lola.

"Jack?" moaned Clare. "Again?"

"What's he *doing*?" said Theo.

Clare was watching Jack, who was watching the otters. He slowly pulled a slingshot out of his back pocket and lifted his arms.

"Stop!" she screamed.

The mama and her babies slid back into the water. They were so quick that Jack didn't have time to pull the slingshot's thick rubber band. Clare covered her face with her hands and felt weak with relief that the otters had gotten away.

"Was he planning to *slingshot* them?" said Theo.

"Who would *do* that?" said Lola.

Clare stared at Jack across the water. "Someone who is bored or lonely or disturbed?"

"Or all of the above?" said Theo.

Jack stared back at her. "Oh, hey there, City Girl. How ya doin'?"

Even though she felt like turning away, Clare forced herself to keep eye contact. *If he thinks he can stare me down because I'm not a boy, or because I look small or weak, he's wrong. I've been treated like that before, and I won't let it happen again.*

"Leave the animals alone! They aren't bothering you at all!" shouted Clare. She wasn't used to yelling at people—except her mom, maybe. She wanted to leap up and shake her fist at him, but she was afraid of flipping the canoe.

"You tell him, Clare," said Lola.

Jack rolled his eyes. "Whatever. They're just otters. I'm *so* over you guys."

As he turned around, Clare thought she heard him mutter, "Gay moms . . . blind dogs . . . What next?"

Jack pushed his boat back toward Lake Lyons, tripping in the grass twice before getting it into the water. "Alwyn was better before you all got here!" he yelled as he started rowing away.

Clare forced herself to take a few deep breaths. "Is he always like that?"

"Ever since we moved to Alwyn." Theo shrugged. "I don't know what he was like before we got here."

"Maybe Jack should join Drama Club. He could star in our next tragedy." Lola fluttered her eyelashes and placed the back of her hand along her forehead like an actress in a soap opera.

"Karma," said Clare.

"Karma?" said Theo.

"When you put good energy into the world, it comes back to you. And when you put bad energy into the world, it can come back to you, too," said Clare.

Theo stroked his chin. "Interesting."

"What're you saying?" said Lola. "That someday Jack will realize how stupid he is and face some terrible consequence?"

"No," said Clare, "I mean, I hope not." She wasn't exactly sure *what* she meant. Grandpa Anthony had always talked about karma, and she liked the idea of it. It made her think of a compass, pointing her toward what was good and true, regardless of what others were—or weren't—doing. "Somehow, I think things balance out in the end."

Fifteen
The Kids

The next day, Clare tried to push the image of Jack and his slingshot out of her mind. "Why would he *do* that?" she whispered to the urn. "Is he a bully, or does he just make really dumb choices, or both?"

Later, when her mom asked if she wanted to go for a drive, Clare was glad for the distraction. "Sure. Where to?"

"Nowhere special." Her mom's expression was unreadable. "Well, that's not true. I'll tell you when we get there."

"Is Grandma Lulu coming?"

"Nope. Just you and me." She put a finger over her grinning lips. "Shh. A secret."

Helen told Grandma Lulu that they were heading to the library. Clare did, in fact, need to return a few books, but when she climbed back in the truck, her mom started to drive the other way on Main Street, out into the hills and hollows of rural Alwyn.

Clare looked over at Helen as they bumped along the country road. She squinched her eyes, and in the luster of sunshine, she noticed a thin brown halo covering her mom's scalp. "Um, Mom, are you letting your red grow out?"

Helen's hair had been scarlet—as bright as a candy apple—for as long as Clare could remember.

"Maybe."

"Why?"

"It just seems like the right time to shake everything up."

"I think it'll look great." Clare rolled her window all the way down, and the summer air grabbed playfully at her ponytail and t-shirt. "By the way, you know Grandma Lulu is going to *freak* over this. She'll be so excited. She's always wanted you to go natural."

"What's funny is that she got up really close to my head the other day and gave it a good, long stare. I'm sure that she noticed, but she was *unnaturally* calm about it. I was impressed with her restraint." Helen raised her eyebrows at Clare.

Clare raised hers back.

Clare's mom slowed the truck as they approached a wrought-iron gate along the side of the road.

"We're going to the cemetery?" said Clare. "Why?"

"Wait and see." Her mom turned into the driveway and drove through the gate, which was wide open. She parked in a small lot next to a chapel.

"We're like the only ones here," said Clare.

"Even better. Come on!"

Clare followed her mom as their feet crunched on the gravel. They walked to the top of a sloping, grassy field, which was speckled with faded, old headstones that were gray, brown, and white. Their once-shiny surfaces were embroidered with lichen and moss.

Clare loved the rustic hodgepodge feel of the cemetery. "It's so pretty."

"Isn't it? I want to take you to see the kids."

"The kids? Mom, I don't see *anyone* around here, especially any kids."

Her mom laughed. "They aren't actually kids. I think Dad called them that out of affection." She pulled Clare over to a pair of matching headstones. "Meet my grandparents—your great-grandparents."

Clare bent down to trace their engraved names with her finger. *Jake Andrew Burch. Dorothy Elizabeth Burch.*

"Grandpa Jake was a country doctor, and Grandma Dorothy was a nurse. They drove all around the Northwoods, carrying their black leather medical bags with them. They were the last generation to make house calls." Clare's mom brushed dirt and weeds from the two headstones. "Hi, kids."

"Grandpa Anthony used to bring you here to see them?" said Clare.

"Ever since I was a little girl. This is the first time I've been here without him. It's strange, but it feels good to carry on the tradition with you, now."

"Hi, kids," said Clare. "Nice to meet you. I bet Grandpa Anthony loved you as much as I loved him. Actually, my grandpa was loved by . . . *everybody*." She remembered how well-attended his funeral service had been. Friends, neighbors, and patients had filled every row in the church.

Her mom pulled a dandelion from the grass. "Grandma Lulu and I ordered your grandfather's headstone yesterday. We'll scatter his ashes in the lake like he asked, but he wanted a stone here, too. I think it'll look nice next to the kids.'"

"Oh," said Clare. A marker at the cemetery felt so concrete and inescapable, like there was no turning back. She trailed her hands through the blades of grass and tried to imagine what the new stone would look like there. She felt her eyes filling. Why couldn't she go back in time, so they weren't sitting in a cemetery in the first place? "If only I . . ."

"If only you *what*? Listen, Clare, it was incredible how you took care of him and stayed with him as long as you could. You were tough and smart, and you did more than anyone could've expected. Plus, you did it alone, with no help."

"But I wish I'd been faster!" Clare put her head in her hands. "I wish I hadn't gone numb! I feel like I let him down."

"You didn't let him down. He had a blockage in his heart that was big and sudden, and nothing would've helped him. Grandma Lulu and I have told you that so many times, but you have to believe it deep inside so you can move forward."

"I know." Clare didn't like to admit that her mom was right, but she couldn't deny that she *did* want to move forward, like an ant taking a tiny step on a peony blossom.

"Maybe being in Alwyn for the summer will help," said her mom.

"I think it already is," said Clare.

"I'm glad to hear that." Her mom stood and dusted off her knees. "Hey, there's something else I want to do while we're here. Something that your grandpa and I did when *I* turned thirteen." She grasped Clare's hand, and together they walked back to the parking lot.

Clare couldn't remember the last time she'd let her mom hold her hand in public. *I never would've let her do it in Morrissey*, she thought. *But in Alwyn it feels right.*

When they got to the truck, Clare moved to the passenger side door, but her mom shook her head.

"Nope. I'm getting in on your side. You're getting in on mine."

"What?"

"You heard me. Climb in." Clare's mom walked her around to the driver's side and opened the door. "I'm teaching you how to drive."

Sixteen
Onward

Clare thought her mom was kidding.

"Come on, get that perplexed look off your face!" said Helen. "It's *fun*. This cemetery is the best place to learn how to drive. No one's around, and there's zero traffic. There aren't any stoplights, either."

"Our ideas of 'fun' might be a little different, Mom," said Clare. "You think it's fun to stay home on a Friday night and grade art projects."

Helen ignored her. "Your grandfather taught me to drive here when I became a teenager. My driver's ed classes were a breeze a few years later because I already knew everything."

Clare tipped her head. "Does Grandma Lulu know that you brought me here to do this?"

"Gosh, no. She never knew that Dad brought me

here, either. It was our secret—but not a bad one, since we weren't hurting anyone or doing anything wrong. I was hoping it could be the same way with you and me." Helen looked at Clare with an expression that reminded her of Roger's face when he thought he might get a treat.

"Um, OK, but I think it's sort of crazy."

"Get in, then!" New wisps of baby brown hair frizzed around her mom's face.

"I don't know what I'm doing, though, and this truck is gigantic. What if I crash?"

"You won't crash. And the anticipation of something is a lot worse than the thing itself, so let's stop thinking about it and just *do* it." Helen showed Clare how to adjust the seat so her feet would reach the pedals. She pointed to the ignition and showed her how to insert the key. "Go ahead. Switch it on, now."

Clare turned the key, and the truck rumbled to life.

They buckled their seatbelts.

"We need to back out of our parking spot first," said Clare's mom. "You have to be looking all around to see what's behind you. Look in the rearview mirror, in your side mirror, out my window, and now turn your head so you can look out the back window."

Clare thought that was *way* too many places to be looking, but she did it anyway. There were still no cars or people around, which was a relief. She shifted from park to reverse.

"Now lift your foot, gently, and press on the accelerator."

The car went backward. Clare couldn't believe that she was directly responsible for the movement.

"Great. Now shift from reverse to drive. Let's take the road that goes through the cemetery. It's such a pretty drive."

Clare wasn't sure if the trembling in her body was from nerves or from the engine itself. She knew she needed to figure out a way to push the accelerator hard enough so that the truck would move, but not so much that she'd gun it. She wriggled her toes inside her sneakers, thinking of all the starting blocks they'd curled around. Her feet had never let her down before.

"Keep scanning your mirrors and windows so you know what's around you," said her mom.

"OK." Clare scanned everything she could.

"Get used to the way the truck moves. I know it's big, but you're high up. That gives you a good vantage point for seeing everything around you. Also, don't forget to breathe. It'll help you stay relaxed. Loosen your grip a little bit, too."

Clare glanced at her knuckles and saw that they were white. She attempted to relax her fingers, but she was trying really hard to keep the truck in the center of the narrow road. "I'm afraid I'll get too close to the grass on either side and knock into a headstone."

"You're not going to knock into a headstone. You're staying centered, and you're taking the curves nicely. Not too fast and not too slow. You're totally getting the hang of it! Isn't it exciting?"

Clare didn't answer. She proceeded to drive the cemetery loop, again and again. Each time they passed by her great-grandparents' gravestones, she and her mom called out, "Hi, kids!"

Eventually, Clare felt her shoulders fall, so they weren't bunched up by her ears anymore. *I think I love this,* she thought. *I like the feeling of being in control and having all my senses working. I'm noticing things I never would have otherwise.* Like the way the truck absorbed some of the bumps when she drove through a rut. Like the chipmunk that darted across the road. Like the vibration of the engine deep in her abdomen. These sensations filled her with a boldness she didn't know she had.

"Mom?" Clare blurted out.

"Yes?"

"Are you glad you had me?"

"Of *course* I'm glad I had you. Why would you ask that? Especially right now, while you're driving for the first time?"

"I guess I'm picturing you doing the exact same thing when you were my age, which makes me realize that I've never really thought about what your life was like before I came along."

"Oh," said her mom. "Well, I'm glad to tell you anything you want to know."

"You were really young when I was born." Clare swallowed. "Haven't I made it impossible for you to have friends and *fun*?"

"What do you mean?"

"Back in Morrissey, all you do is teach. You never hang out with anyone your own age, and you just seem . . . crabby. I've always figured it was my fault."

Clare's mom made a *pfft* sound. "Maybe I need to explain some things. And thirteen seems like the age when you're old enough to understand."

"Thanks," said Clare. *Wow*, she thought.

"You know that your dad and I met in college. We got married pretty quickly, much to your grandmother's horror."

"Why was she so upset?"

"She wanted me to follow my passions, and study painting in Europe, and have a ton of friends—just like her. She didn't want me to limit myself."

"But that doesn't sound crazy," said Clare.

"No, but at the time all I wanted was to have a beautiful wedding in the backyard, which is what Henry and I did. Soon afterward, he got sick. Things happened very fast." She sniffled.

Clare wanted to look over and see if her mom was all right, but she knew she couldn't tear her eyes from the road.

"I found out I was expecting you around the same time that he was diagnosed with his blood disease," her mom went on. "He passed away a month before you were born."

"I already know how he died, Mom," said Clare. "You've been telling me that story since I was little. I guess I wanted to know more about *you* and how you got by afterward."

The car was quiet.

"Like, weren't you lonely?" said Clare, a minute later.

"Of course," said her mom. "I missed Henry so much, but I had Mom and Dad. They were at the hospital when you were born, and I moved back home so they could help me raise you. You and I have never been alone."

Clare nodded. *I don't have a brother or a sister, but I've been able to grow up in the same house as my grandparents, which is pretty amazing,* she thought. "But, Mom, what about friends?"

"Well, unfortunately, I didn't give a lot of attention to my other relationships after I met your dad, and over time they fell away. I thought Henry was all I needed to be happy. When he was gone, I didn't have any friends left, so I said to myself, 'Who needs other people, anyway?' and then I acted like I didn't. It became my truth. I've been just fine without friends."

Clare raised her eyebrows. "You've been *just fine*?" She wanted to make air quotes around the words, but she couldn't let go of the steering wheel.

Her mom sighed. "Well, no. I just acted like I was."

"Oh, Mom." Clare didn't know what else to say.

"It's easy to ignore my loneliness when I stay busy. The more tasks and projects on my to-do list, the less time I have to think about it."

"But I can see how happy you are, now that you've got Abby and Marisa! You're always doing fun stuff with them. You get coffee on Main Street and exercise at Abby's boxing gym and go fishing together. Isn't it great?"

"It *is* great. Your grandmother's been on my case for more than thirteen years to have a social life. I should've been doing it all along." Clare's mom rubbed her hands over her eyes. "I can't believe I'm admitting that. Please don't tell her. It'll go right to her head."

"I won't." Clare laughed. "But I think *you* should. It would probably mean a lot to her."

Her mom nodded.

Clare liked the idea of the fault lines between her mom and Grandma Lulu filling in forever.

"Did you and Grandpa Anthony talk like this when he was teaching you how to drive?" she asked.

"Oh, yes. I don't know what it is, but there's something about being in a car that gets people talking."

"I thought it would be depressing hanging out in a cemetery, but it isn't—in summer, at least. Maybe in the middle of winter it's not so great." Clare tried to remember the stark shapes and colors of that grim, icy season,

105

but she couldn't. She felt lightyears away from its barrenness.

"You'd be surprised. Cemeteries can be beautiful in winter, too."

"I guess," said Clare. "Maybe you can get used to anything, if you give it a chance."

"Even driving." Helen grinned.

Clare grinned back. Meanwhile, the road ahead of her unfurled elegantly into countless green knolls beyond.

"Onward," she whispered.

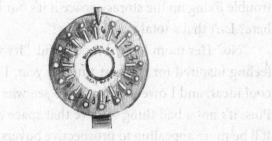

Seventeen
The Bounty

When it was time to leave the cemetery, Clare was surprised at how hard it was to climb out of the driver's seat. She would've driven home if her mom had let her.

As Helen pulled into the driveway at the cabin, Clare noticed a bunch of rags and cans of paint stacked alongside the garage. "What're you doing up in the storage space, anyway, Mom?"

"I've been cleaning it out, bit by bit. It was a pigsty."

"And now you're going to paint it?"

"I already finished. I decided to convert it into an art studio. It gets great light, and there's plenty of room for me to spread out my supplies and canvases."

"So . . . you're feeling creative again?"

"I'm getting there."

Clare crossed her fingers. "But why go to all that

trouble fixing up the storage space if it's our last summer here? Isn't that a total waste of time?"

"No." Her mom looked thoughtful. "It's worth it. I'm feeling inspired for the first time all year. I've got some cool ideas, and I owe it to myself to see where they lead. Plus, it's not a bad thing to have that space all tidied up. It'll be more appealing to prospective buyers."

Clare closed her eyes. She couldn't picture someone else living in Grandpa Anthony's cabin.

In *their* cabin.

"Is there anything I can do so Juliet doesn't have to sell it?" said Clare.

"At this point, I think it would take some sort of miracle to change your grandmother's mind," said her mom. "I'm devastated, too, Clare. My preference would be to keep it. But look at it this way—Grandma Lulu is adjusting to life without Grandpa Anthony, just like you and I are. We're all doing it in our own way. She hasn't been coming up north every summer like we have, so she doesn't have the same strong connection with Alwyn. And I know she's concerned about money. How can we pay for repairs and taxes and everything? She's just trying to be smart about it."

Clare opened her eyes. "I could apply for a job! Like, a real one! Then I could help with the money."

"You're not old enough." Her mom patted Clare's shoulder. "And if anyone should be doing something to improve our finances, it's *me*. If I could just sell some paintings, then I could finally establish myself as a professional artist." She frowned as she opened her car door. "But I have to actually paint something first."

Clare climbed out of the truck. "You will, Mom. I know it."

"That's my goal," said her mom.

I guess I'm not the only one with goals this summer, thought Clare. *I hope both of us can accomplish what we set out to do, or it'll be tough to go home in August—and never come back.*

"Hi, Grandma Lulu!" shouted Clare as they walked inside the cabin.

No one answered.

"Grandma Lulu, where are you?"

"Her car's in the garage, and she's not out walking the dog," said her mom, bending down to scratch Roger's floppy ears.

Clare peered out the great room window. "She's not on the deck or the dock. And the fishing boat and canoe are still tied up."

Clare heard the muffled sound of a car door closing.

Softly, slowly Grandma Lulu scampered inside.

Clare had to do a double take. She couldn't believe this lady wearing a Chicago Cubs baseball cap was her grandmother. Where were the high heels and lipstick? Where were the oversized earrings and jangling bracelets?

Gone, thought Clare.

When Grandma Lulu noticed Clare and Helen standing there, watching her, she stood up straight. "Why, hello, girls!" Two plastic bags thumped against her legs.

"What've you got there, behind your back?" said Clare.

"Nothing."

There was a thud as one of the bags tumbled to the floor.

"Rats," said Grandma Lulu.

"Is that a bag of . . . pork chops?" said Clare.

Before Grandma Lulu could respond, the second bag tumbled to the floor. She smiled sheepishly.

"Is that a bag of . . . chicken drumsticks?" said Helen.

"Grandma Lulu, what's going on?" said Clare.

"Darn it. I was hoping to keep this as my little secret."

"Keep *what* as your little secret?" said Clare.

"Well, Nedd and Lloyd Vogel called me up and asked if I wanted to go with them to a meat raffle. They thought I'd have fun, you know, trying something new and different—something with a local flair."

"How is it possible that I've been coming up north my whole life and have no idea what a meat raffle is?" said Clare's mom.

"I can't believe your father never told you about them, Helen," said Grandma Lulu, throwing up her arms. "What was he *thinking*?"

"I guess he was too focused on fishing," said Clare.

"Why'd you want to keep your meat raffle a secret?" said Helen.

Grandma Lulu pursed her lips. "I'm aware that I can be a little high maintenance . . . but look at me now! I'm winning pork and chicken at a meat raffle! I thought you'd tease me."

"We wouldn't tease you," said Clare.

Helen barked with laugher. "Maybe *you* wouldn't, Clare, but *I* might."

Clare covered her mouth and giggled.

Grandma Lulu shook her head. "It's fine. Poke fun at me all you want, but for the record, it's organic, locally raised pork and chicken. We'd be paying a fortune for it back in Morrissey."

Roger, who had been sniffing the bags of meat, flapped his tail.

"How does a meat raffle work, anyway?" asked Clare.

"Nedd and Lloyd took me to a tavern over in Boulder Bay. It was packed with guys. There were only a few other ladies there, but I didn't mind. No one paid any attention to me because all they cared about was winning the meat. It was a dollar a paddle. I purchased a few, because why not increase my odds?"

"Sure," said Clare. "Why not?"

"The paddles were numbered, and the organizer had a big wheel, like in a game show. He spun it, and whatever number the arrow landed on was the winner. He did a few rounds, and I won *twice*. Can you believe it?"

"I certainly cannot," said Clare's mom.

"I've never won anything before, darlings. Naturally, everyone applauded, although I'm sure they were envious of my bounty."

"I've got to hand it to you, Mom," said Helen. "You're turning into a real Northwoods gal."

"I think it's cool you're trying new things," said Clare.

"Thank you for noticing how far I've come," said Grandma Lulu.

"But what are we going to do with all this meat?" Clare shooed Roger away from the plastic bags. "It's way too much for the three of us."

"Why don't we invite the Porters and Vogels over for a cookout on the Fourth of July?" said her mom. "We could have a party and grill out. It'd be fun."

While Helen and Grandma Lulu reorganized the freezer to make room for the two big packages of meat, Clare skipped over to the urn. It was still on the mantle, as if perched on a throne.

"Grandma Lulu's going to meat raffles, and Mom's making social plans," she whispered. "Who would've guessed?"

She appraised the urn.

"*You* guessed, didn't you?"

She didn't need the urn to answer the question for her.

"Then maybe you *also* guessed that I'd make friends

in Alwyn, and swim every morning, and learn how to musky fish with the Vogels."

She leaned in a little closer and added, "But what about my goals, Grandpa Anthony? Do you think I'll accomplish all of them before summer ends?"

The urn stared back at her. Clare knew it would reveal nothing.

"Well," she said, brushing her hand across the burnished wood, "I won't stop trying."

Eighteen
Not Much Smaller
Than an Eighth Grader

Clare texted Olive and Emmy the next afternoon. *Bobb, Nedd, and Lloyd are taking me out for another musky lesson.*

Any luck catching one yet? asked Olive.

No, but there's a lot to learn. It'll take a while for me to know everything.

Emmy sent back a cartoon of a fish so big that it had snapped a fishing rod clean in half. *LOL. This'll be you someday.*

Hope so, texted Clare.

She grabbed her musky rod and tackle box from the garage and met the Vogels on the dock. They were loading up the Burches' fishing boat with their impressive collection of gear.

There are definitely advantages to being taught by the owners of a bait shop, thought Clare.

"Hop in, Kitty-Clare!" hollered Lloyd. He settled into the back seat and started the motor.

Clare clipped on her life jacket.

"Are you fellas ready to go, or no?" Lloyd called out to his brothers.

"You betcha." Nedd climbed in the front seat.

Bobb sat next to Clare in the middle row.

Lloyd puttered away from the dock. "All righty then, where're we headed?" He looked right at Clare.

"You want *me* to decide?" she said.

"Let's see what you've picked up from our lessons so far," said Nedd.

"Well, um, OK." Clare thought for a minute as Lloyd chugged out into the lake. "I think we should go to the northeast corner, where it's really shallow."

"Why?" said Bobb.

"Because the muddy bottom of that part of the lake is dark, which means it attracts sunlight and holds more warmth than the deeper waters. So, right now, the aquatic plants and seaweed growing there are coming in fast and thick."

"And?" said Bobb.

"All those plants and seaweed attract the smaller fish that muskies like to eat."

"And?" said Bobb.

"There might be some muskies there, hunting around for a snack," said Clare.

"Thatta girl," said Bobb.

Clare felt her cheeks flush, and she knew it wasn't from the sun.

When they arrived in the northeast corner, Lloyd switched off the motor. In the silence—which really wasn't silence at all, because Clare could hear birds and bugs and waves and the breeze—Bobb helped her string up her musky rod. "Which bait would you like to use today, sweetheart?"

Clare poked through her tackle box. "A Super Plopper." She extricated one, careful to not snag or pierce her skin on the sharp metal hooks dangling from it like a pair of treacherous earrings. Painted neon green, yellow, and orange, the lure was long, plastic, and shaped like a torpedo. At the end was a rotating rubber tail.

"Excellent choice," said Nedd. He attached a Super Plopper to the end of his own line, too, but his was painted silver and black.

"What can you tell me about topwater baits?" asked Bobb.

"Well," said Clare, "it means that after I cast out my line, I'll let it sit on top of the water for a few seconds, and then I'll begin to reel it in. As the Super Plopper comes back to me, the tail will spin like crazy. It'll splash and gurgle along the surface of the lake like a real fish, which will hopefully attract a musky."

"Righty-o," said Lloyd.

When Clare's Super Plopper was secure on her line, Bobb handed the rod back. It was deceptively solid, and thick enough so that it wouldn't break, like the picture that Emmy had texted.

"Why don't you stand on the seat, Clare? Be careful, now." Bobb held out his hand to help her up.

Clare stared ahead into the muddy waters. *Are you out there, muskies?* She hefted up her rod and cast out her line. Her Super Plopper sailed through the air with a sizzle and landed in the lake with a *plunk*. She waited until the ripples dissipated—one, two, three, four, five seconds—then reeled the lure back in. It bubbled and spattered through the water, just like she knew it would.

Come on, muskies. I'm trying to arouse your interest, wherever you are. Pay attention! Look at my pretty, shiny, fluorescent-colored lure! Go ahead, take a bite!

"Keep your pace steady," said Bobb. "Don't forget to do your figure eight, now. Make it fast and strong. Give those fish one last chance to get excited about your lure."

When her Super Plopper was a few feet away from the boat, Clare angled her rod so the tip was in the water. She made a big figure eight with it, once, twice.

"Nice little flourish," said Nedd.

"Thanks," said Clare, but she didn't get a bite. She pulled up her rod and cast a second time.

With his own rod, Nedd followed the same steps as Clare: cast, wait, reel, figure eight. He didn't get a bite, either.

They went through the process again, but this time, something exploded in Clare's peripheral vision. She turned her head in time to see a dappled silver and green beast lurch up from the seaweed toward Nedd's lure. She almost dropped her rod. She couldn't believe the length and bulk of the creature trying to ambush his Super Plopper.

"I've got me a follow!" yelled Nedd.

"Oh," panted Clare. "Oh, my gosh."

"It's a musky, sweetheart!" said Bobb. "That's the real deal!"

"But . . . he's *huge*. And *alive*." She blinked—and blinked again. She'd seen mounted replicas of trophy muskies hanging on the walls of the bait shop and at Dutch's, but a breathing, writhing musky was a completely different story.

"Real nimble for a submarine, ain't he?" Bobb cackled.

The musky whipped his tail, showing off his ghostly-pale underside. For a fleeting second, he looked like a gigantic *S*, and then he vanished into the vegetation and mud.

"Aw, geez," said Nedd.

"Sorry, brother. Guess he wasn't in the mood for a snack," said Lloyd.

"How *big* was that thing?" Clare managed to say.

"At least three feet long. Probably more. Not much smaller than an eighth grader," said Bobb, with a wink.

But Clare didn't wink back.

What was I thinking? she wondered, sinking down onto her seat.

I was way *too ambitious, wanting to catch a crazy fish like that.*

Nineteen
The Treasure Hunt

That night, Clare's head hit the pillow like a bowling ball. As she fell asleep, she pictured the musky in her mind. She saw its flat head, long snout, and vicious teeth—and she shivered. The last thought she had was, *I don't think getting near one of those things is a very good idea.*

But when she woke up the next morning, her first thought was, *Still my goal!*

She threw on her swimsuit and paused by the urn as she walked out of the cabin. "Muskies might be the freakiest animal I've ever seen," she said, "but I'm going for it, Grandpa Anthony. You're not here to catch one yourself, but *I* am. It's my last summer in Alwyn, and I'm going to do it, for myself and for you." She tapped the top of the urn and went outside to do laps.

120

Later, after she'd finished, she lay with Roger in the yard, which was speckled with the sunny faces of hundreds of dandelions. The buzz of cicadas surrounding them was a riotous, perpetual whirr. Over the last week, she, Lola, and Theo had begun to find the insects' dried-up shells stuck to the trunks of trees. She knew that when they matured, they split their skins down the middle and pushed themselves right out. They left behind hollow husks that looked like old, outgrown clothes.

Clare watched Roger snuffle around the yard. He pushed his nose into the grass and snorted. Then he flipped over and began rubbing his back in the same spot, squirming from side to side like a wriggly nightcrawler.

"Hi, Roger! Hi, Clare!" Theo came running down the lawn, with Lola behind.

Roger sprang to all fours and bounded in the direction of Theo's voice, his ears flapping like laundry on a clothesline. Theo dropped to his knees so Roger could find him. Roger pounced into his lap and started licking Theo's face and arms.

"That tickles!" Theo shrieked. "Gosh, do I love you, Roger. You're the best little blind dachshund I know."

Clare waved away the mosquitos, which were threatening to dive-bomb Theo and Roger for a snack. "That's what my friend Emmy in Morrissey always says. Between the two of you, he's the most spoiled dog ever."

"Can we give him a treasure hunt?" asked Theo.

At the mention of *treasure hunt*, Roger stood stock-still.

Lola giggled. "He's so smart. He knows exactly what you're saying."

"Sure," said Clare. "Let's give him a treasure hunt."

This sent Roger into a frenzy. He sprang off Theo and yowled.

Ever since Clare had shown Theo what a treasure hunt was, he'd been obsessed. "Roger's going to get chunky from so many treats," she'd said, but she let Theo organize them anyway. She knew they helped Roger feel more self-assured and independent as he moved throughout the cabin.

In the kitchen, Clare gave Theo a small bowl of dog treats that smelled like salmon and liver.

"The stinkier, the better," said Lola. She held out a bowl of her own for Clare to fill.

Theo and Lola hid the treats in places that Roger could easily sniff out: under the kitchen table, inside a sneaker, behind a chair. Then they watched Roger rummage through the great room. He found each one, gulping them down so fast that Clare hoped he wouldn't choke.

"Good job, buddy," said Lola when Roger was done.

Roger thwapped his tail against the rug as if expecting a second round.

Clare laughed and told him no.

Theo, meanwhile, had turned his attention to the mantle. "Is it upsetting to have that box around, Clare?"

"The urn? No. It's the opposite, really. It's just my grandfather. I like knowing he's in there. I . . . talk to him. Is that crazy or what?"

"I don't think it's crazy at all," said Lola. "I talk to my birth mom and birth dad all the time."

"You do?" said Theo.

"Sure. It's not a big deal."

"But how?" said Theo. "They're in South Korea."

Clare wondered the same thing.

"I know they couldn't give me the life they wanted me to have," said Lola. "They wrapped me in a soft blanket when they took me to the orphanage, which I think was their way of showing how much they loved me. Whenever I want to talk to them about something, I go in my bedroom and lock the door and just talk to my blanket." Lola pointed at her brother. "Now don't you make fun of me, Theo."

"I won't," he said, with a solemn look on his face. "I promise."

"I'm glad I'm not the only one who speaks to inanimate objects," said Clare.

"Will it be hard to empty?" asked Theo. "The ashes, I mean?"

"Yes," said Clare, "but I think I'll be OK."

"I bet it was really hard to lose him," continued Theo. "Do you ever want to talk about it with me and Lola?"

Clare shrugged. *Maybe soon.*

Theo reached out and squeezed Clare's fingers.

She squeezed back.

Lola wrapped her own hand around Clare and Theo's so their fingers were all connected like a complicated pretzel.

"Do you ever talk to your birth parents, Theo?" asked Clare.

"No, but I think about them a lot, and I wonder what they're like," said Theo. "I'm sure I've got the same eyes and skin color as them, so even though they're not here with me, they're *in* me."

"What about you, Clare?" said Lola.

"What do you mean? I wasn't adopted."

"I know, but what about your dad?"

Clare paused. "Well, he got really sick with a blood disease and passed away a month before I was born. I never got the chance to know him, so I'm not sure of all the ways we're connected. I know he loved books and had hazel eyes, just like me. But it kind of feels like I have a space inside me that will always be empty."

"Me too," said Lola.

"Me three," said Theo.

Clare rubbed Roger's head. "Maybe everybody in the world has an empty space, somewhere inside them."

"But that's not a bad thing," said Lola. "I think mine gives me my fabulous dramatic abilities."

"I think mine gives me my curiosity," said Theo, thumping his chest.

"I've never thought about it that way before," said Clare. She placed her own hand over her heart and thought about the two big empty spaces inside. One for her dad, and one for her grandfather.

Then, just like Theo, she thumped her own chest, yowling like a jungle creature and sending them all into a fit of laughter.

Twenty
The Revelation

A few days later, it was the Fourth of July.

Clare looked around the campfire. The flames were throwing shadows on the faces of the people she'd grown to love so much, in such a short amount of time. *A few months ago, I only knew the Vogel brothers a little bit, and I had no idea that the Porters existed! Now here I am, celebrating the Fourth of July with all of them like one big family,* she thought.

She shoved a s'more in her mouth and wondered why they were always too tall. A shower of graham cracker crumbs fell in her lap.

For dinner, they had stuffed themselves on Grandma Lulu's meat raffle pork chops and chicken drumsticks, along with eggplant, blueberries, green beans, corn on the cob, and watermelon. Grandma Lulu had wanted to pluck a tomato off their plant, which was growing inch by inch, but Clare told her to wait a little longer. "Maybe in August, Grandma Lulu. It takes a while for the little bulbs to fatten up and turn bright red. We shouldn't pick them before they're ripe."

Now, the Burches, Porters, and Vogels were sitting together under a dome of stars. Clare was listening to everyone's laughter, and to the popping of logs, and to the clamor of voices carrying through the dusk. *Hanging out around a campfire is a lot like being in a car*, she thought. *It sure gets people talking.*

To her right, Helen was telling Abby and Marisa about a painting she was working on. Her voice was rising in apparent excitement. "I'm not ready to show it to anyone yet, but I'm moving in the right direction, and I might even turn it into a series of paintings. My only challenge is that I've got a blank space that I haven't been able to fill. I have to decide what to do with it."

Figure it out, Mom! thought Clare. She loved that when her mother was working on a canvas, the exasperated little "V" between her eyebrows would unstiffen, and her entire face would smooth itself out. *Please keep on creating something new, because I really like this version of you.*

To Clare's left, Grandma Lulu was talking to Bobb and Nedd. "I need to put together a list of the repairs that have to be done before Juliet can put the cabin on the market."

"Don'tcha worry," said Bobb.

"We'll help," said Nedd.

Ugh, thought Clare. *I'd be thrilled if I never heard Juliet's name again.*

On the other side of the fire, Lola, Theo, and Lloyd were laughing about Roger, who'd managed to burrow his whole body into the front pocket of Theo's sweatshirt.

"Sweet doggy," said Theo.

From inside Theo's pocket, Roger sneezed.

Roger's been so happy in Alwyn, thought Clare. *I'm not sure he'll want to go back to Chicago when August is over.*

She chewed her lip. *What about me?*

She couldn't believe she was asking herself the question.

Two months ago, I was panicking about living here for the whole summer. Now, I have new people and things in my life that fill me with happiness. I feel like I belong up north as much as I do in Morrissey, which will make things even harder at the end of summer.

She pushed another marshmallow onto her roasting stick.

If I could snap my fingers and have Emmy and Olive here, then I'd be happy in Alwyn, for always.

She poked her marshmallow into the flames.

Well, not PERFECTLY happy.

For *that* to happen, she would need to have Grandpa Anthony there, too. Alive and healthy. And she knew that was impossible.

For the first time in a while, Clare's mind reverted to the if-onlys that had plagued her all winter and spring, like a swarm of bloodthirsty mosquitos.

If only I'd been paying better attention.

If only I hadn't been lost in a book.

If only I'd been in the kitchen, helping to get ready for the party.

Clare pulled her softened marshmallow out of the fire. It was the perfect shade of golden-brown, just the way she liked it. She waited for it to cool and then tugged it off her stick.

She thought about Grandma Lulu and how she'd given Alwyn a chance.

She thought about her mom and how, after a long dry spell, she was pushing herself to bring something new to life.

And then there's me. I've made two new best friends, and I'm swimming like crazy, and I'm learning how to fish for muskies. Mom even taught me how to drive the truck. If I can do all that, why can't I do this other thing, too?

Clare's marshmallow fell from her hand and landed under her lawn chair. She was glad Roger was curled up with Theo, or he would've gobbled it up.

I can, she decided.

"Hey . . . everybody?" she said to the circle around her. "I need to tell you something."

The circle around her grew quiet.

"I need to tell you something so that I can . . . move forward. It's important."

Just start at the beginning, Clare Burch.

She blinked her eyes closed, and just like that, it was late afternoon on December thirty-first.

"It was New Year's Eve, and I was reading on my bed," she said. "*Anne of Green Gables.* I was sort of lost in my own world."

Clare's mom had wanted to finish up some grading at school, which Grandma Lulu had complained about—extensively. "What other teachers are working on a holiday? The answer is *none.* You should be putting on a cute cocktail dress and going out with friends, Helen!" she'd hollered.

Her mom had left anyway, and then Grandma Lulu had gone out, too—to pick up the steaks she'd ordered for the party she and Grandpa Anthony were hosting.

"Grandpa Anthony was in the kitchen making appetizers or something," continued Clare. "Roger was with him. I'm sure he was waiting for scraps to fall on the ground so he could wolf them up."

Theo patted the lump in his sweatshirt. "Good boy."

Clare had been completely absorbed in the adventures of Anne Shirley when she noticed a tapping sound. *Is someone at the door? How long have they been knocking?*

She chucked her book aside. The tapping got louder.

Roger whined. He sounded frightened. "What is it? What's wrong, buddy?" she called out.

She ran downstairs, yelling her grandfather's name. There was no response, but there he was, lying in a heap on the kitchen floor. His skin had a grayish tinge to it, and his breathing was shallow. He was tapping his fingers on the floor. Clare knew he was trying to get her attention. "I'm here! I'm here, Grandpa Anthony!"

Roger's barking was like an alarm clock that she wanted to turn off but couldn't. She dropped to the ground and put her palm on Grandpa Anthony's forehead. It didn't feel right. "What is it? What's wrong?"

He didn't answer.

"What should I do?"

"Heart attack," he wheezed.

"Oh," she said. "Oh."

She reached in her back pocket for her phone, but it wasn't there. *It must be up in my room, somewhere on my bed! Do I stay here with Grandpa Anthony or go get help?*

She dragged herself to her feet, her knees knocking into each other. "I need to find my phone so I can call nine-one-one," she finally said. Her words sounded like they were coming from a different room.

"I must've stood there for five minutes," Clare told everyone around the campfire. "I was frozen. I couldn't make my body work. It's like I was stuck in a jar of peanut butter." Through the squiggly waves of heat rising from the campfire, she could see expressions of kindness on everyone's faces. It gave her the strength to continue. *Onward*, she thought.

Clare told them how she stumbled upstairs to search for her phone, which she finally found wedged under her pillow. Her fingers were rubber, and it took a few tries before she could use them to press the right numbers. She couldn't remember anything about the phone call, but somehow she exchanged information with the operator and made it back down to the kitchen. On the floor, she pulled Grandpa Anthony's head into her lap, waiting for the ambulance to arrive.

Hurry, hurry, hurry.

Roger ran in a frantic circle around them, panting and crying.

Clare tried to shush him, but she was more focused on stroking Grandpa Anthony's face, just as he had always done to hers. "It's going to be OK," she whispered. She trailed her fingers from his temple to his jawbone, over and over. Her hand seemed so small, as if she were looking at it through the wrong end of a telescope. "I'm here, and I won't leave you."

Grandpa Anthony smiled. "I know," he whispered back.

And then the paramedics were there, and they lifted Grandpa Anthony onto a stretcher. Clare followed them outside into the biting cold, wearing no shoes or jacket, and one of them told her no, she couldn't ride with them.

"I'm not leaving Grandpa Anthony," stammered Clare, but the paramedic didn't seem to hear. He pushed her aside with his meaty arm. They were taking her grandfather to the hospital, he said, and she should go there later, with an adult who could drive her.

"There aren't any adults at home right now," said Clare, louder this time. "No one can drive me. I'm not leaving him."

The paramedics lifted the stretcher into the ambulance, and Clare clambered in behind. Her bare feet slipped on the chilly metal step, but she didn't stop.

"You're not supposed to be in here," the paramedic snapped. He waved his hand in her face as if she were a fly he wanted to shoo away.

"I'm not leaving him!" shouted Clare.

He rolled his eyes. "I *cannot* deal with this drama today."

"Just let her come," said another paramedic. "There's no time to argue."

The angry one climbed out and slammed the door. He jogged around to the front of the ambulance and got in the driver's seat.

As they peeled out of the driveway, Clare tried to make herself as little as possible. She didn't want to get in the way as the paramedics pulled out the defibrillator, which was loud and terrifying and made her grandfather's body jerk like he'd been plugged into a light socket.

"The whole thing was like a scary movie," Clare told everyone. "I felt like I couldn't function."

"But Clare," said her mom, "you *did* function. You were the one that called for help, and you even got yourself inside the ambulance."

Everyone nodded.

"It just didn't feel like enough," said Clare.

During the ambulance ride, her jaw began to ache as she clenched her teeth. She thought it would somehow keep her from wailing, but she heard whimpers escape her mouth anyway. She climbed onto the stretcher next to Grandpa Anthony and clutched his hand.

The nice paramedic patted her back. "You're brave. You shouldn't be here. It's no place for a kid, but your grandfather's lucky to have you with him."

"You *are* brave. The paramedic was right," Theo blurted out.

"I think I would've just covered my eyes and cried like a baby," said Lola.

Clare shook her head. She needed to finish her story. *I never want to hear the if-onlys rattling around my head again. They've been in there too long, and they've used up too much of my energy. It's time to be done with them, forever.*

Grandpa Anthony was still conscious, but she could

feel him slipping away. He pulled his hand out of hers and placed it on top of her head. It felt like a warm knitted cap. "It's going to be a new year," he said. "Make it a great one."

"Yes," murmured Clare.

He took another breath, and she leaned in closer.

"Make it a great life."

Yes, yes, yes.

Clare gripped his hand again and refused to let go until they arrived at the hospital and he was taken away from her forever.

The nice paramedic wrapped Clare in a blanket and carried her out of the ambulance. He tucked her into a quiet corner of the hospital, while a nurse picked up the phone to track down her mom and Grandma Lulu.

"And . . . that's my story." Clare's breath felt a little raggedy, but other than that, she was still in one piece. *I did it.*

She hadn't even told Olive and Emmy all the details of what had happened to her on that awful day. It had been too much, too soon.

"Gosh, sweetheart. You really rose to the occasion," said Bobb.

"You sure did, Kitty-Clare." Lloyd nodded his head so emphatically that Clare hoped he wouldn't give himself whiplash.

"I'm so glad you stood up to that paramedic," said Abby, raising a fist.

"I never met Grandpa Anthony," said Theo. His glasses reflected the brilliant firelight as he leaned toward Clare. "But it sounds like you really channeled him. You stayed calm and did all the right things, just like when we go fishing."

Clare wiped her eyes with the back of her hand, depositing smudges of melted marshmallow along her cheekbones. She'd never thought of herself in any of the ways her friends had just described. She'd spent so many months wishing she'd been faster or better that she'd missed the point. She'd done everything she could; she had been enough.

"Darling, I've been trying to tell you for *months* that nothing could have saved your grandfather," said Grandma Lulu. "You could've moved at the speed of light, and it wouldn't have made a difference."

Clare nodded. "I know." She felt like a garden hose that had been turned off. The very last drops of blame and doubt trickled out of her, and she was blissfully empty.

"Why did it take so long for you to accept all of this?" said her mom, gently.

Clare stared into the fire, which felt like it was starting to burn the soles of her flip-flops.

"I guess I wasn't ready." It was the most honest answer she could give. She kicked off her flip-flops, which were, in fact, beginning to melt. She pulled her legs up onto her lawn chair and hugged them tight.

Crossing the Pressure Line

The reason was crystal clear.
I just needed to cross the pressure line first.

Twenty-One
The Dive

In the days following the Fourth of July, Clare felt as serene and untroubled as the wispy cloud-curls in the sky above her.

Telling my story of what happened on New Year's Eve was like accomplishing a goal I didn't even know I had, she thought.

Clare closed her eyes and listened to the lake, feeling grateful for every surge and swell—and for Lola and Theo, who were sprawled out beside her on the raft.

Streams of water ran down their warm bodies. Clare could hear each of them breathing deeply after the laps they'd just done—*bonus* laps for her, since she'd already done her regular training that morning.

But then Lola roused Clare with a jolt. "Are you kidding me?" she hissed.

On the shore, Jack was getting off his bike. He wore a pair of swim trunks, and around his waist was an inflated yellow inner tube.

"Why's he here?" said Clare, sitting up.

"And why is he wearing an inner tube?" said Theo.

They watched as Jack let his bike fall to the grass. He walked to the end of the Burches' dock and dipped a toe in the water. "Great day for a swim, ain't it?" He plugged his nose with his fingers and jumped into the shallow water. He began to doggy paddle toward them.

"You don't have to let him come out here, you know," said Lola. "It's your dock and everything, and you can tell him to leave."

Clare shrugged. She wasn't sure exactly what to do, but she kind of wanted to give Jack one last chance to just be nice.

When he got to the raft, he struggled to grasp the ladder and climb up.

Clare began to twirl the rubber strap of her goggles. She watched them spin around her outstretched finger, just so she wouldn't have to look at him.

"It's a lot easier when you don't have an inner tube attached to your body," said Lola.

"Oh, shut up." Jack pulled himself onto the raft. He stood up and flicked lake water onto them. "That ought to cool you guys off. You were looking a little hot."

Theo wiped the drops off his glasses.

As Jack made a show of getting comfortable next to them, Clare tried to catch Lola and Theo's eyes. She wondered if they should swim back to shore. *But I don't want to*, she thought. *I belong here. This raft belongs to me.*

She whirled her goggles so fast they almost flew off her finger.

Plus, I don't just leave when things get difficult.

Jack looked at the sky. He pointed to a few crows flying in big loops above them. "Don'tcha think those birds are obnoxious? They never stop cawing. They're loud and dirty, and they eat roadkill. They're real lucky I left my BB gun at home, or I'd pick 'em off, one by one." He aimed an imaginary BB gun. "*Bang, bang, bang.*"

"They might be loud, but they're communicating." Clare didn't care that she sounded like a nerdy professor giving a lecture.

"Whatever," said Jack.

"Crows are smart," she continued. "They have large brains for their size, and they're almost as intelligent as chimpanzees. As for eating roadkill, they keep streets clean by eating dead animals that would otherwise rot and make a mess."

"Well," said Jack, "I guess you must know it all, coming from Chicago and having a fancy dentist in the family and everything."

Clare felt anger surge through her, just like water rushing through the culvert. She wondered how Jack even *knew* about her family in the first place, but then she reminded herself that she was in Alwyn. Things got around fast up north. "Leave my grandfather out of this."

"Sure thing," said Jack. "That's real easy since he's not alive anyway."

The only sound was the lapping of waves against the raft.

"Why would you come out to the raft—*my* raft—just to try and make me feel bad?" Clare surprised herself, jumping in before Lola and Theo could say anything themselves.

"Because it's so easy." Jack shook his head as if the answer were obvious. "Especially when you don't belong here. I mean, why don't you just go back to Chicago? And Lola and Theo can go back to Milwaukee or China or wherever they're from."

Enough, thought Clare as she stood up. She felt ten pounds lighter as the words shot from her mouth like cannonballs. "GET. OFF. MY. RAFT."

"Make me." Jack had gotten to his feet, too. He tussled with the inner tube, which squeaked as it rubbed against his damp body.

Clare flapped her arms just as she would for swim team warm-ups. She took a few steps backward and charged toward Jack. She pushed him off the raft as effortlessly as dropping a wad of tissue in a garbage can.

141

Jack was a streak of yellow as he coasted through the air. He smacked the lake, spluttering and splashing.

"Let's go," said Clare, snapping her goggles into place.

Lola and Theo were silent.

Clare turned to them. They were gaping at her. "Guys?" she said.

"That was spectacular!" said Theo.

Lola shook her head. "I didn't know you had it in you!"

"Beat him to shore?" said Clare.

Theo slid his thick tortoiseshell glasses into the zippered pocket of his swim trunks and leaped off the raft, with Lola close behind. They sent their spray in Jack's direction.

Clare tucked the toes of her left foot over the raft's edge. She crouched, stretching her arms forward. As Jack was sputtering and shouting, Clare imagined that his voice was the buzzer at a swim meet. She pushed off the raft, calling all of her muscles into action. She exploded upward and outward, creating a perfect arc over his head.

"What the . . . ?" he said.

Clare made contact with the water a few feet beyond him. She rose to the surface and knew she'd just done the best dive of her life.

"Just wait!" Jack shouted at her from behind. "I'll get you back!"

As her arms and legs shifted into a front crawl, Clare considered her strength objectively. She was fast, and her limbs moved in harmony with each other.

I'm not a failure—and I've never been one.

"Go ahead and try," she yelled at Jack as she came up for a breath. "I can handle anything."

Twenty-Two
The Solution

From inside the cabin, Clare, Lola, and Theo watched Jack wade out of the lake and get on his bike. The yellow inner tube gradually, sadly deflated as he pedaled back down the driveway.

"It felt amazing to stand up to Jack," said Clare, "but he looks so pitiful."

"I sort of feel bad for him," said Theo.

"You do?" said Lola. "Why? He *chooses* to make it hard for anyone to be around him."

Clare didn't know what to think.

As Jack disappeared down the road, she heard a rumble of thunder. She poked her head outside and saw that the gathering clouds were tinged with violet. They looked like they'd been whipped into angry ribbons with a gigantic butter knife.

"We gotta go, Theo," said Lola.

"I'm sure Mom or Grandma Lulu would drive you guys home," said Clare, "but Grandma Lulu's at the market, and Mom's out on some nature hunt."

"Nature hunt?" said Theo.

"Something for her painting." Clare shrugged. Helen had been going out every day with a basket slung over her arm. She'd filled the basket with pinecones, blades of grass, and the fuzz of white dandelions, but she complained that she still hadn't found the right way to fill in her painting's empty space.

"We'll be fine," said Lola. "It'll only take a few minutes to get home on our bikes."

As Theo unzipped his backpack to pull out his windbreaker, Clare thought she saw animal fluff inside.

"Um, Theo," she said, "what's *in* there?"

He reached in and pulled out a tuft of bird feathers. Some of them were sleek and downy, others were stiff and coarse.

"Seriously, Theo, are you keeping an aviary in your backpack or what?" said Lola.

"No, I'm not keeping an aviary in my backpack, Lola. I just like looking for feathers. They're all over the place, if you open your eyes. Of course, it helps to wear a suitable pair of glasses." He tapped his tortoiseshell frames and grinned.

"Where did you find all of them?" asked Clare. "Do you know what birds they came from?"

"I found them in the grass, and by the lake, and in the woods. All over, really." Theo fanned his treasures in his hands. "This striped one is a turkey feather. If you slide your finger down the side, it feels just like teeth on a comb." He pointed out the feathers that had come from bald eagles, hawks, and loons.

"And *that* one is from a crow," said Clare, pointing. She would know that gleaming indigo-black color anywhere.

"Yep," said Theo.

"They're beautiful," said Clare.

"Aren't they lovely, Lola?" Theo waved the feathers at his sister.

"Yes, they're lovely. Just keep them out of my face," she said, brushing them away.

Clare tapped her chin. "How many feathers do you have?"

"I've got like ten here, and probably another twenty at home," said Theo.

"Are you planning on doing anything with them?"

"No," he said. "No one really cares about feathers—"

"I do!" said Clare.

"Me too," said Theo, "but I just collect them for fun."

"Is there any chance you'd want to share them with my mom?"

"Sure, she can have as many as she wants. Why?"

"I have an idea," said Clare.

146

Theo patted the feathers into a fuzzy pile and handed them to Clare. He hollered goodbye along with Lola as they left the cabin.

While changing out of her wet suit in the bathroom, Clare realized she hadn't been keeping close tabs on her mom's artistic progress like she normally did. Back in Morrissey, her mom's studio was located in a spare bedroom, and Clare loved peeking inside every so often to see how her paintings were coming along.

I've been so into my own goals and friends this summer, I haven't even gone up to see her new studio, she thought.

The downpour started as soon as Clare left the cabin. Beads of rain smacked her skin as she waited for the garage door to go up. She hoped Lola and Theo had made it home all right.

Once inside, Clare wiped her face and pulled Theo's feathers from under her t-shirt. They were damp and crumpled, but she smoothed them with her fingers, and they sprang right back into place. *I love how birds can handle the weather. They might get soaked during a storm, but they always dry out and are OK.*

With the sound of rain beating against the garage like a snare drum, Clare eyed the stairway leading up to the storage space. The last time she'd climbed the steps, she'd been with Grandpa Anthony, helping him organize his gardening tools.

When she got to the top, she gaped at the space in front of her.

Once dingy and gray, the walls and plank floors were bright white, which made the room feel much larger. Her mom had removed all the old equipment from Grandpa Anthony's shelves and worktable, and she'd neatly arranged her art supplies on top of them. There was a utility sink in the corner of the room for cleaning brushes, and Clare could smell the bottles of turpentine that were sitting next to it. Her mom had even rigged up new lighting. Before, the space had had one dim bulb hanging from a cord, but now, there were lamps everywhere. Clare snapped on the nearest one so she could see what was resting on her mom's easel.

"Oh, wow," she breathed.

The canvas was undoubtedly a work in progress, but Clare thought it looked amazing. The pigments her mom had used were the very colors of the Northwoods. They were the same hues of the trees, grass, lake, and sky—but even more vivid and saturated. *They're like Alwyn, but on vitamins!*

The canvas was unlike anything Clare had ever seen. It wasn't a traditional landscape or still-life; it was spirited and plucky and confusing. Clare liked the way it made disorder feel orderly.

Behind a shape that resembled a cloud, she saw the faint outline of her own face. She sensed Grandma Lulu's curls in the movement of the grass, and Grandpa Anthony's eyes in a mist of water. The tree trunk was the same shape as Roger's slim body, and a red flower made Clare think of her mom's dyed hair.

Maybe I'm just imagining it, but I think my whole family's in there.

Clare saw there was a gap in the painting, too, a blank spot that seemed to be begging for some sort of resolution. "I bet this is it—the empty space Mom was talking about." She cleared a spot on the worktable for the feathers and poked around for a scrap of paper.

Hi Mom, these feathers are for you. They're from Theo. He's got more and will give them all to you if you want them.

You've definitely found your creative spark.

xx Clare

"Actually . . ." said Clare. "Forget leaving a note. I'll tell her face to face. It's too important." She gathered up the feathers.

Before turning back to the stairway, Clare stood before the easel one more time. Her eye snagged on something she hadn't noticed before. In the upper-left corner of the painting was the moon, still lingering, even in the scene's broad daylight. Clare peered closer.

How did I miss this?

Veiled by the shadows, domes, and rilles of the surface of the moon was the face of her father. She moved toward the canvas, and his expression seemed to quiver and vibrate in response. If she had been able to put her hand directly on the daubs of paint—which she didn't dare, since they might still be wet—she was sure she'd feel an actual current of energy.

Even though I never got the chance to know him, he's still a part of us. Of me.

His shadowy shape and luminous colors would always be in the background of her family. He wasn't as far away as she'd assumed; she just needed to look more closely.

And for the first time, Clare felt OK with being a wad of play dough.

Life is messy and confusing and sad, she thought.

But it can be beautiful at the exact same time.

Twenty-Three
The Bouquet

Clare was reading on the couch when her mom returned from her nature walk.

Helen stood just inside the door, her clothes clinging to her body. She flung the empty basket she was holding to the floor, where it landed with a soggy thud.

Clare set her book down. She wasn't sure if she was dealing with her new mom or her old mom. It appeared as if Helen might yell, or cry, or laugh, but Clare didn't know which. "Are you . . . OK?" she asked, as Roger burrowed under a blanket next to her.

Helen flicked her tangle of half-red, half-brown hair out of her face, sending drops of water everywhere. Clare wondered if she should get up and find a towel, but her mom held up a hand.

"A failure!" she yelled. "I'm a failure!"

151

Old mom, thought Clare, closing her eyes. *Maybe I should count to ten like parents do when their toddlers are having temper tantrums.*

Helen kicked the basket, which was so waterlogged that it was beginning to resemble oatmeal. "I've collected all the nature I can find for my paintings, but nothing is working. Not pinecones. Not grass. Not dandelions. I have to figure this out, or . . ." She put her head in her hands and moaned.

"Or what, Mom? You're feeling creative again, right? Isn't that what matters?"

"Yes, but it's more than that." Helen looked at Clare with anguish. "I decided to make an entire collection of paintings and hold an art show during Musky Days."

Alwyn's annual festival was coming up in August, right before they were scheduled to go back to Morrissey, but Clare didn't understand what an art show had to do with it. "But I thought Musky Days was all about pig roasts and fish fry competitions and the Mister Musky parade?"

Helen flapped her hand. "Yes, of course, it's all those things. But there will be so many people in town, I thought it would be the perfect opportunity to put myself out there professionally. I've been working with Marisa, because she's a business expert and everything. She found an old, unused storefront just off Main Street, and she rented it for me. I can hang all my paintings there and show them off to a big crowd and maybe even try to sell them."

"But that's so great!" Clare sat up straight.

"Not if I can't get my paintings done!" wailed Helen. "I'll never finish my Northwoods series if each of them has a huge blank space. How *ridiculous* I am. I never should've set such a massive goal for myself."

Clare leaped off the couch and ran into her bedroom while Roger began to howl from under the blanket. When she got back to the great room, her mom had sunk to the floor, a puddle forming around her. Clare handed her the note she'd written up in the studio and then the feathers, which she had arranged in a mason jar, like a bouquet.

Her mom stared at them without making a sound.

Clare chewed her lip, waiting.

"Clare Burch!" shouted Helen, scrambling to her feet. "These are the solution! You're brilliant!"

"Well . . ." Clare didn't feel especially brilliant, she just wanted to be helpful. She would do anything for Helen to feel fulfilled—not simply because her mom was happier that way, but because they all were.

Helen threw her arms around Clare and squeezed so tightly that she lifted her right off the ground. "And there are more? Feathers, I mean?"

"Theo's got a bunch at home, and he said you can have them all."

Her mom set Clare back onto her feet and began to laugh. "Why didn't I think of feathers? They're everywhere, but I never noticed. The answer was right in front of me the whole time. I just needed to look more closely."

Clare cocked her head. *Yelling, crying, AND laughing.*

She giggled as a fresh round of thunder reverberated through the cabin.

She'd never understood her mother so well.

Twenty-Four
The Library

The rain dragged on for days.

I'm going crazy.

Clare stared forlornly at the drops going *splat* against the great room window.

I can't swim. I can't fish. I've only got four more weeks of summer, and I still have two goals left. At this rate, I won't accomplish either of them.

"Goodbye, darling. I'm heading off to another meat raffle with Nedd and Lloyd," said Grandma Lulu, throwing a purse over her tan shoulder.

"Can you win us some ground beef this time?" Clare kissed her grandmother's cheek. "Then we can eat tacos and cheeseburgers every night until we go back to Chicago." She didn't know if she was kidding or serious.

A car horn beeped in the driveway. "Must run!" said Grandma Lulu, blowing kisses.

Helen followed closely behind. "I'll be up in my studio if you need me. I've got lots of painting to do."

Clare sighed and watched the raindrops trickle down the glass. *If I have to be stuck inside another day, I need a new library book.*

Like an answer to her wish, the rain let up a little. Clare checked the forecast on her phone and saw that the weather would be dry for at least an hour. It was her chance.

She found Roger sleeping in a laundry basket full of clean clothes and rubbed his head. "Be good, buddy. I'll be back soon." She tossed on her backpack and bike helmet, and she was off.

...

As Clare eyed the novels on display at the library, she reminded herself not to be greedy; everything she chose had to fit in her backpack. She ended up picking *A Tree Grows in Brooklyn*, because, according to the back cover, it was a "beloved classic." She flicked the novel open to a random page, and her eye landed on a sentence: "There had to be the dark and muddy waters so that the sun could have something to background its flashing glory."

Clare lifted her eyebrows. She knew all about dark and muddy waters.

She tucked the book under her arm and began to hunt for a second one. As she rounded one of the tall bookcases, she ran smack into a librarian. "Oh, I'm sorry!"

"It's all right. May I help you find something?" The librarian had long, wavy strawberry blond hair and big brown eyes.

"Sure, I guess," said Clare. "Maybe something nonfiction?"

"What topics are you interested in?" asked the librarian.

"Well, I like to swim."

"Perfect. Seven hundred and nineties. Let's go." The librarian led Clare through the aisles of the Dewey Decimal System until she kneeled and pointed. "Diving, marathon swimming, synchronized swimming, and any other water-related sports activity you can imagine."

Clare pulled a few books off the shelf. "This one looks good." It was about American swimmers—all of them women, all of them Olympians. She paged through it, studying the photographs. Pride, elation, and disappointment—all of it was there, shimmering on the swimmers' faces.

I don't know if I'll ever go to the Olympics, but I think I understand how they feel, she thought.

"Lots of ups and downs," said the librarian, peering over Clare's shoulder at the page.

Clare nodded.

"Francie Nolan faces some big ups and downs, too." The librarian gestured at *A Tree Grows in Brooklyn*.

"Francie Nolan?" said Clare. "Oh, I don't know anything about that book. I just randomly chose it."

The librarian smiled. "I think you'll like it. It's a beloved classic."

Clare laughed. "That's what the back cover says."

"Why don't we get you checked out, then?"

Clare glanced out the window. It hadn't started raining again, but she needed to leave soon to avoid the next round of showers. "Thanks."

After the librarian swiped her card at the circulation desk, Clare stashed the books inside her backpack and said goodbye. As she headed out of the building, she noticed a plaque on the wall, right next to the front door. She'd always rushed by it before, never pausing to take a look. The plaque consisted of a wooden rectangle, with an engraved metal plate and photograph mounted on top.

IN MEMORIAM
Jillian Wilson, Librarian.
For her years of selfless service and loving
dedication to the Alwyn Public Library.
She is deeply missed.

Clare screwed up her face as she scrutinized the photo of the librarian who was deeply missed. Had Jillian

Wilson been friends with the nice librarian who'd just helped her? She had a pretty smile and was standing with what Clare assumed was her family. There was a man on her left, and a boy on her right. Clare let out a sharp little gasp. The boy was Jack.

"*What?*" she whispered. So many things felt instantly clear to her, and so many things felt even more confusing.

Jack.

Jack Wilson.

I didn't even know that was his last name.

Clare realized there were so many things about Jack that she didn't know. She winced as she put on her backpack and walked outside.

Maybe I shouldn't have given up on him so fast.

Twenty-Five
The Present

As she biked home from the library, Clare thought about Jack. She didn't know what it felt like to lose a mom, but she figured it was one of the worst things that could happen. *It's probably a huge part of who he is. No wonder he's so full of anger. And I actually pushed him off our raft! I'll never be able to make it up to him.*

The storm began to nip at her heels as she turned into the driveway. By the time she made it inside the cabin, the rain was pounding away. Clare slipped off her sneakers and called Roger's name. He hadn't greeted her with his usual round of yips and sneezes, nor was he in the laundry basket. "Where are you, little guy?"

As Clare changed into dry clothes, she heard a whine from under her bed. She got on her hands and knees, and there was Roger—just as the cabin shook from a roll of thunder. "Are you scared of the storm, buddy?"

He gave a half-hearted twitch of his tail.

"It's OK. You're not alone anymore."

In the tight space, he rolled onto his side.

She gave him a quick rub on his belly. "Come on out, now. Let's find a spot to snuggle. I've got two new things to read—*A Tree Grows in Brooklyn* and a book about Olympic swimmers."

Clare carried Roger into the great room. Not for the first time, she noticed how different the cabin looked, compared to when they'd arrived in June. It was tidy and shiny. Stylish, even. Grandma Lulu had put a new rug in the center of the room. She'd replaced the battered couch with a leather sofa, which she'd topped with a jumble of bright throw pillows. She'd even hung up some of Helen's old paintings.

And somehow, all the updates seemed to go perfectly with Grandpa Anthony's trophy fish on the walls.

"I hope you'd approve of all the changes around here," Clare said to the urn. "It's still the same cabin, but way comfier."

But then she grimaced. "I bet it's Juliet who's telling Grandma Lulu to make all these improvements, so it'll sell faster. I keep hoping that Grandma Lulu will change her mind."

Clare put Roger on the floor and went into the

kitchen to look for Grandpa Anthony's *Smile! I'm a dentist!* mug. She came back and placed it right next to the urn. "This is one thing we'll never say goodbye to, no matter what."

Roger leaped up onto the couch.

Clare marveled at his act of faith: to be blind yet still unafraid to jump. "Way to stick your landing, little guy."

She walked over to the bookcase and picked up one of the photographs that Grandma Lulu had framed and placed around the room. It was a selfie, taken a few weeks before, of Clare, her mom, Grandma Lulu, and the Porters. Their faces were bathed in sunshine, and their mouths were open in laughter. They were on the deck, and behind them was the tomato plant.

"It's become a monster," Clare said to the urn. "Seriously. It doesn't matter what the weather is like, or if we remember to water it or not. It just keeps growing." She imagined the juicy tomatoes they'd finally be able to pluck from it, in a matter of weeks.

"*Everything* seems to be growing these days. In all different directions."

Clare eyed the urn suspiciously.

"Is *that* why you wanted us to spend a whole summer up north together?"

I always knew my grandfather was smart.

She placed the photograph back on the shelf and trailed her finger along the spines of Grandpa Anthony's novels, biographies, and memoirs. They were arranged neatly, just like books at the library. She thought about how she, her mom, and Grandma Lulu would have to box up them all up and move them to Chicago, along with everything else in the cabin.

Her finger paused on a paperback. It was small and understated, and it looked completely out of place in the row of big, bold hardcovers.

"*Sweeping Up the Heart*?"

Confused, she slid the novel off the shelf.

"This looks like *my* book."

And then she remembered: she'd brought *Sweeping Up the Heart* to Alwyn with her the summer before. She'd loved the quiet, bittersweet story so much that she'd finished it in an hour or two. After she closed the cover and wiped her eyes, Grandpa Anthony had asked if he could borrow it.

"But this is a middle grade book, and you're . . ."

"Old." He winked at her. "It doesn't matter. Good literature can cross lots of borders. I'm eager to read a novel that's affected you in such a big way."

But now, Clare wasn't sure if he'd ever ended up reading the book. They hadn't talked about it. *I'll never know.* She felt like crying.

She started to page through the novel. To her relief, it was immediately clear that Grandpa Anthony *had* read it. He'd left his customary trail of underlined sentences and folded-back page corners. In the middle of *Sweeping Up the Heart* was a receipt from Bobb's Bait Shop for leeches, jigs, and a bag of Gummie Balls. Farther on, she found a Caramel Dot wrapper flattened between the pages. She smiled as she lifted it to her nose. It still smelled like chocolate.

Toward the end of the book was a sheaf of papers that had been folded and tucked inside. She opened the sheaf and froze.

BOOKS THAT CLARE BURCH NEEDS TO READ

"Oh," she gasped. "Wow." She flipped through the pages. They were covered with Grandpa Anthony's handwriting.

Clare pushed Grandma Lulu's new pillows aside and threw herself on the leather couch next to Roger. He yawned and rearranged himself.

She clasped the pages in front of her. Six, she counted. Six pages of titles, authors, and comments, all compiled by her grandfather. Based on the dates he'd jotted next to each book, he must've started the list right after Clare was born.

"How'd you do this without me ever finding out?" she asked the urn.

The first book was *A River Runs Through It* by Norman Maclean. Grandpa Anthony had noted that it was about nature, fly fishing, and family tragedy. "*Builds* character and empathy. This one's a must-read when you're a little older."

She nodded. She would read anything he wanted her to.

The last book was—of course—Kevin Henkes' *Sweeping Up the Heart*. "*This is my favorite kind of story: unassuming, crisp, and filled with heartache and hope,*" her grandfather had written. "*Thanks for introducing me to a novel I wouldn't have read otherwise. I need to start borrowing more of your books!*"

"This is the best present I've ever gotten," she said to the urn. "Now I'll always have ideas when I go to the library."

She went through the list more closely and, midway through, couldn't believe her eyes when she saw *A Tree Grows in Brooklyn*. "No way! I literally just checked this one out." She raised an eyebrow at the urn. "What are the odds?"

"*This book feels like a good friend,*" her grandfather had written. "*Although it's been around for a long time, it's still fresh and impactful.*"

She wondered if that's what it meant to be a beloved classic.

"*With her quiet fortitude and keen awareness of her surroundings, Francie reminds me of you, Clare.*"

"Oh." Clare had never been compared to a literary heroine before. "Thanks, Grandpa Anthony." She couldn't wait to read the book and try to see herself from this perspective.

Roger grunted and rolled over.

Clare leaned forward to place the sheaf of papers on the coffee table. She was thinking so hard about the ways she and Francie might be alike that she almost didn't notice the folder poking out from underneath the newspaper. She flicked the newspaper aside and picked up the folder.

"Oh, no . . ."

She felt like a fishing lure that had just been cut from its line.

She was sinking, sinking, sinking, into the depths below.

Arranged inside the folder was the paperwork, signed and dated, to officially put the cabin on the market.

Twenty-Six
The Change of Plans: Part I

"I can't believe you're *really* selling the cabin!" Clare cried as she and Grandma Lulu bumped along the bike trail the next afternoon.

They pedaled through a stand of Norway pines. The trunks were so dark and ramrod straight that they reminded Clare of a life-size barcode.

"Can I do *anything* to change your mind?" wailed Clare.

"Darling—"

"I've come up north every summer of my life," Clare went on. "The cabin is a huge part of who I am. I thought it would feel bad or weird without Grandpa Anthony here, but in some ways it's actually *better*. I mean, you, me and Mom all *belong* to each other now, and that never would've happened if we'd stayed in Morrissey. I would've been at the pool all the time, and Mom would've been working too much, and you would've been busy with shopping and tennis and getting facials and—"

"I completely understand," said Grandma Lulu.

"But if you completely understand, then why did you hire that ghastly Juliet to sell it?"

"You've got a long history with Alwyn that I don't have." Grandma Lulu tucked a loose blond curl under her bike helmet. "I get overwhelmed when I think about all the energy that's required to own a cabin in the North-woods when one lives six hours away."

Clare choked down a sob. "But it's not like you have a job or anything! Couldn't you make time for it?" She didn't want to sound bratty, but she was feeling desperate.

Grandma Lulu braked and put her feet down in the dirt. "Let's walk our bikes for a minute. It'll be easier for us to talk."

Clare wiped her eyes as she climbed off.

"It's funny you should mention me not having a job," continued Grandma Lulu.

Clare cringed. "I'm sorry, that wasn't nice of me to say. I know your life is just the way you like it, and—"

"Well, actually, that's not true. There's always room for new adventures, and that's another reason why I'm selling the cabin."

"I don't get it. What do you mean?"

"You know that Anthony and I met in college. He was

in dental school, of course, but were you aware that I was a business major?"

Clare shook her head. She hadn't given much thought to what Grandma Lulu had been like before becoming her grandmother.

"I had straight A's and dreamed of working for a big, fancy advertising firm on Michigan Avenue."

Clare had a sudden vision of a bustling office downtown. She imagined Grandma Lulu wearing her posh French tweed suit, presiding over an important meeting with a pencil stuck jauntily behind her ear.

"Anthony and I wanted to get married," said Grandma Lulu, "but I couldn't work for a big, fancy company if we lived in the Northwoods, so we decided to stay in Chicago."

"And then he opened his dental office in Morrissey?" Clare pictured Grandpa Anthony's trays of orderly, stainless steel instruments, and the bendy lights for peering inside patients' mouths.

Grandma Lulu nodded.

"Did you get your job downtown?"

"No."

Clare looked over at her grandmother and noticed a miniscule tremble in her chin. For the first time, she wondered if there had been a different path for Grandma Lulu. A path she hadn't chosen.

Grandma Lulu went on. "Soon, I was expecting Helen, and then I was busy raising her. It was a change of plans, but I adapted."

Clare stopped walking, the truth dawning on her for the first time. "And then *I* was born, and you were busy raising *me*. I messed up all your dreams!"

"Nonsense, darling. You messed up nothing. You're the very best part of my life!"

Clare shrugged helplessly. "But what does any of this have to do with selling the cabin?"

"I've decided to get a job when we go back to Morrissey," said Grandma Lulu. "I'm not sure what I'll do yet, but I've started researching my options. I really hope you can support this big change. I won't have nearly as much free time as usual."

Clare could tell by her grandmother's face how excited she was. "Of course I'll support you, Grandma Lulu. It'll be strange not having you at home all the time, but I'll be fine."

Grandma Lulu reached out and squeezed Clare's hand.

There's officially no hope left for keeping the cabin, thought Clare. She would never go against her grandmother's dreams.

But then, Grandma Lulu let out a piercing shriek. She yanked at Clare's arm, sending her stumbling against her bike. "Good glory!"

"What?" Clare's helmet had slipped over her face. She pushed it back and raised her eyes. "What's wrong?"

Standing directly in front of them was a bear.

Twenty-Seven
The Caramel Dots

The bear was jet-black. It batted around a cluster of wild blueberry bushes like they were Grandma Lulu's throw pillows on the new couch. Scrabbling for the sapphire morsels, it shoved them greedily in its mouth.

Clare couldn't tear her eyes away. The bear was like an apparition or a magic trick. But she knew it probably wasn't a great idea to hang around. "I think we need to go," she whispered.

Grandma Lulu looked dumbstruck.

"We need to go," Clare whispered again. "I don't know if that's a male or a female, but if there are babies nearby, we could be in trouble. Mama bears don't like people getting too close to their little ones. Do you think we can try to turn our bikes around?"

"What if . . . what if it eats us?" said Grandma Lulu.

"Black bears don't eat humans," said Clare, but she wasn't positive about that.

"Can it see us?"

"I'm not sure." Clare remembered from a book she'd read that although bears were nearsighted, they had excellent senses of smell and hearing.

As if on cue, the bear reared away from the blueberries. It turned toward them and stood up on its hind legs.

"Oh, no," Grandma Lulu whimpered.

"Don't panic." Clare tried to take a slow, deep breath. *I've been in an emergency situation before,* she reminded herself.

The bear's fur was so fluffy that Clare thought it looked like a stuffed animal. But then it snorted and coughed, and she was reminded that it was very much alive. "I can't remember if we're supposed to run, shout, or jump up and down," she said. *Come on! Think!*

She briefly wondered if this was New Year's Eve all over again—freezing in place, not knowing what to do, losing every scrap of her bravery.

The bear tipped onto all fours and shuffled toward them. Its stride was flat-footed and clumsy, but Clare knew it could run faster than a horse if it wanted to.

The bear scrunched up its eyes and stared at Clare.

She scrunched up her eyes and stared back. She could feel a river of sweat rolling off her body.

"Go!" Clare shooed the bear away. She could hear a tremor in her voice, but she kept going. "Go away, now!

You've got other things to do! I've heard there are some nice raspberries over there." She pointed randomly toward a cluster of aspen trees.

The bear snorted again.

"Did you hear me? Raspberries! Yummy raspberries! The last ones of the season! Over there!" She jabbed her finger even harder toward the aspens.

After a moment that seemed to stretch on and on, the bear turned around and retreated into the woods, heading in the direction of Clare's made-up raspberries.

After the snapping of branches and the crunching of leaves subsided, the bike trail fell silent. It seemed impossible to Clare that a wild animal had just been *right there*, nibbling on a snack.

Next to her, Grandma Lulu panted.

"We're OK," Clare told her.

"Are you sure?"

"I'm sure." Clare glanced at her grandmother, who looked slightly unhinged. *Emergencies can do that to a person.*

"I should've set a fourth goal for myself this summer," she said. "Protect myself and my grandmother from bears." She felt like laughing hysterically.

"You stayed so calm!" said Grandma Lulu. "I would've lost my mind if you hadn't been here with me."

"Well, thanks, but I think it helped that we didn't have any food on us. Bears just want to eat."

Grandma Lulu covered her face with her hands.

"Good glory, Helen was *right*. Thank goodness I was wearing practical shoes! What if we'd had to run for our lives?" She shook her head. "Please don't tell your mother I just said that. It'll go right to her head."

"I won't," said Clare, "but I think *you* should. I know it would mean a lot to her."

"I will, but can we get out of here first?"

Clare tightened her helmet and tried to adjust her shorts, which had gotten twisted up around her waist during the commotion. As she stuck her hands in her pockets to straighten them out, she felt something squishy and warm.

Oh, no.

She'd totally forgotten.

Earlier that day, she'd shoved a bunch of Caramel Dots in her pockets. She loved it when they got all soft from being so close to her body.

I guess we did have food on us, after all!

Clare pushed the Caramel Dots back in her pockets, as deep as they would go.

My little secret—well, mine and the bear's.

She helped Grandma Lulu climb back onto her bike, and then she got onto hers. As she began to pedal, moving cautiously past the blueberry bushes, Clare whispered, "*Thank you, thank you, thank you,*" to the bear.

She trusted the breeze to carry her message along.

Twenty-Eight
The Big Swim

July slipped into August, and suddenly the end of the summer was in sight. Clare noticed that the sun was sinking lower in the southern sky, and that nighttime arrived sooner each evening. Even the cicadas and lightning bugs weren't as lively as they'd been back in June. With each tiny change, the season was getting ready to transition into another.

When Clare thought about packing up and leaving Alwyn for good, it felt like someone had shoved a boulder into her stomach. But then she forced herself to take a few deep breaths. *I'll be OK, no matter what.* She was sure of this because of all the things that had happened to her that year.

She'd been with her grandfather in the ambulance when he died from his heart attack.

She'd said goodbye to Olive, Emmy, and swim team.

She'd made two brand-new friends.

She'd driven the pickup truck without crashing.

She'd learned how to musky fish.

She'd helped her mom figure out how to fill the empty spaces in her paintings.

She'd kept her grandmother from freaking out when they'd run into a bear.

She'd even learned more about the history of her little family and how they all fit together. Snugly, imperfectly, forever.

But there are still a couple things I need to do before I go back to Morrissey.

She would pack as much as she could into her last few weeks up north. She'd make each moment count.

Starting right now.

Clare felt like a porpoise as she cut across the shimmering surface of Lake Alwyn. After more than two months of training, the day of her big swim had arrived.

She'd started off feeling rattled. First thing that morning, Juliet had stopped by the cabin and rammed a garish purple *FOR SALE* sign in the ground. None of the Burches had said a word as Juliet jubilantly shook their hands.

From her library book about Olympic swimmers, Clare remembered that she needed to concentrate on her goal and nothing else: swim to the island and back, in one hour or less, without wearing a life jacket. *That's all that matters right now. Forget about Juliet.*

From the front of the fishing boat, Grandma Lulu held her hands to her mouth like a megaphone. "Keep it up, Clare," she yelled. "You're almost there."

"Honestly, Mom, could you be any noisier?" Helen steered the boat as it chugged through the water. "You're going to frighten away all the wildlife."

"Well, it's not every day that my granddaughter swims all the way to the island, all by herself," Grandma Lulu retorted.

"And back!" Lola added from the middle of the boat, where she was sitting with Theo. "Don't forget she has to swim all the way back!"

"In an hour or less!" Theo waved his hands in the air. He'd used a sparkly silver paint pen to write *GO!* on one arm and *CLARE!* on the other, which made him glitter in the sun.

Just like she'd planned, Clare wasn't wearing a life jacket, but the boat was right next to her if she needed any help along the way.

I've got good form, she thought. *I'm swimming at a constant pace. My breaths are regular. I won't stop until I get to the island.*

Her head bobbed in and out of the water as she continued her breaststroke.

A loon called out from the middle of the lake, its

spooky song silencing the boat. Its mate replied from somewhere just past the island. Their cries were otherworldly and ancient, and even though Clare couldn't see the loons, she could picture their checkerboard backs and inky heads.

A few minutes later, Clare heard Lola ask, "What's *that*?"

"That's an island, Lola," said Theo.

"No, Theo. Look straight ahead at that old dead tree that's sticking out of the water, right next to the island. There's something on the trunk. It's big. *That's* what I'm talking about."

"It's a snapping turtle," said Clare's mom.

"Do snapping turtles really live in Alwyn?" said Grandma Lulu.

"They sure do." Clare's mom cut the motor to the boat.

"Check out its tail," said Theo. "It's like a bumpy, prehistoric-looking triangle."

"Will it attack Clare?" said Lola.

"No," said Clare's mom. "It's harmless. To us, anyway. It just eats plants, frogs, and worms."

Clare's toes had begun to brush against the squidgy bottom of the lake.

Enough about snapping turtles, she thought. "How's my time?" she yelled.

Helen looked at the stopwatch on her phone. "Thirty-six minutes."

"*What?*" shrieked Clare. "It's supposed to be *thirty* minutes! Now I'll have to swim even faster on the way back, and I've already been going as fast as I can."

"Let's pause the stopwatch, now that we're here," said her mom. "Take a quick break, and then we can turn back for the second half of your swim."

The weeds at Clare's feet transitioned into rocks. She sloshed through the knee-high water, trying to avoid the jagged edges of stones. She yelped whenever she stepped on the sharpest ones.

Her mom tossed her a water bottle from the boat.

Clare took a sip. She rolled out her neck and shoulders. She flapped her arms. She thought about how she'd gotten up early every single morning to do laps. She didn't want all of her practice to be for nothing.

Clare could hear the *plonk* of water against the side of the aluminum boat. She wiped her nose with the back of her hand. *Why am I so slow? Why can't I move faster? Two months of training should've been enough to do this swim.*

"You can do it, Clare!" said Lola.

Theo waved his arms in the air again.

Clare threw the water bottle back at her mom.

I love everyone on that boat so much, she thought. *They're so sweet to root for me, but it's the voice inside my own head that matters most.*

Clare's mom switched the motor back on and turned the boat around. "Ready for your second leg?"

Clare snapped her goggles into place. She waded back through the rocks. When there were no stones under her toes, she nodded. "Ready."

Her mom pulled out her phone to restart the stopwatch.

"Set the timer instead, Mom," said Clare. "Set it for exactly twenty-four minutes."

"You sure?"

Clare nodded. "That's all the time I've got, if I want to make it in one hour."

"Take your mark," said Theo.

Clare closed her eyes. She locked her arms by her ears, and she leaned forward, waiting. It felt like the entire world hinged upon the sound that would come next.

"*BUZZ!*" yelled Theo.

She pushed forward and dived into the waist-high water. There wasn't one second to waste.

Her heart pumped. Her lungs took in air and released carbon dioxide in a smooth cadence. She could see the cabin far ahead, its A-frame reaching out to her like the prow of a mighty ship. She fixed her attention on it as she advanced through the water.

"Twenty minutes left!" her mom yelled.

Dragonflies and mosquitos buzzed around Clare's head.

The loons called out again, haunting and eerie.

"Ten minutes!" her mom yelled.

Clare's fingertips tingled. Her muscles felt like they were screaming. She kept swimming.

She thought about the sorrow and blame she'd felt over losing Grandpa Anthony.

You can't catch me.

She thought about the paramedic on New Year's Eve who'd made her feel as insignificant as a piece of lint.

You can't catch me.

She even thought about Juliet's arrogant face and the sign she'd shoved into their yard.

You can't catch me.

"Two minutes!"

Everyone clapped and hollered, and Lola began her high-pitched whistling.

The shore was just ahead of Clare. She felt like she had become her own breath. In and out, in and out. She was all air, whooshing through the lake like a gale.

Everyone on the boat was counting down from ten, and each number seemed to push Clare forward like a hand on her back. The raft was approaching on her right. She transitioned into the front crawl, her quickest stroke, but also the one that required the most energy. She shot forward.

I've done this leg a thousand times this summer.

TEN!

NINE!

EIGHT!

SEVEN!

SIX!

FIVE!

FOUR!

THREE!

TWO!

ONE!

But she hadn't made it in time.

Another ten, twenty, thirty seconds passed by before her slippery, trembling fingers reached out and grabbed the Burches' dock.

She could hear the timer bleating. It sounded like it was mocking her. She wanted to fling her mom's phone into the lake.

I'm always just a little too late.

Too late, too late, too late.

Clare felt herself slipping into a bubbling cauldron of disappointment—but everyone on the boat, except for her mom, who was still steering, jumped in the water and threw their arms around her.

"Why are you congratulating me?" shouted Clare. Her body was shaking like Roger in a thunderstorm. Whether it was from exhaustion, adrenaline, or anger, she wasn't sure. "I didn't do it. I didn't make my goal!"

"You just swam to the island and back with no life jacket in one hour *and thirty seconds*, if you want to get all technical about it," said Grandma Lulu.

Theo shook his sparkly arms in the air.

Clare bent over and tried to get her breath back.

"I'm so proud of you!" her mom yelled from the boat.

Clare fought against the tears welling up behind her eyes. She wrenched off her goggles and wondered why she couldn't feel happier for herself. *You were only a half-minute off your goal.*

"You were so brave," said Grandma Lulu.

"Brave? What does brave have to do with it?"

"Only brave people set fierce goals for themselves, darling."

"Even though—"

Her grandmother shushed her. "Even though you didn't make it in exactly one hour like you wanted. Can't you see the forest for the trees?" She waved her arms at the evergreens and cedars, which stood as tall as church steeples along the edge of the lake.

Clare couldn't help but laugh. Her grandmother looked just like Theo, who was still doing his glittery dance.

None of my teammates in Morrissey could've done that swim as fast as I did, she thought. *They're used to calm pool water that you can see right through. I was in the middle of a lake, which has currents and animals and rocks and plants.*

"I guess I did a pretty good job," she said.

"You certainly did," said Grandma Lulu. "And don't

forget that you can try again next summer. Maybe you can shave off thirty seconds and make it in under an hour, just like you wanted."

Clare tugged off her swim cap. "But we won't be here next summer, remember? This was my one shot."

Grandma Lulu stopped waving her arms. Her face fell. "Good glory, you're right."

Clare looked across the lake and thought of the turtles, loons, eagles, and dragonflies that were out there, going about their day. *They never stop. They don't get to sit around and feel sorry for themselves.*

And then she thought of the swimmers in her library book. Some had trained their whole lives but never won a gold medal. Some had gotten injured. Some had been disqualified before they could even finish their race. But not one of them regretted the time and effort they'd put in. When Clare thought of it that way, she knew her training hadn't been a waste of time.

"There might not be another big swim for me here in Alwyn," she said, wrapping her arms around her grandmother. It felt good to soothe someone else for a change. "But there will be races in other places."

I can be disappointed and sad, she thought. *But no matter what, I have to keep on swimming.*

Twenty-Nine
The Fish of Ten Thousand Casts

The next day, Clare slept in for the first time all summer. Her training was over.

After waking up, she rolled onto her back. *Two months ago, I was dreaming up my goals for the summer.*

She put her hands behind her head and cupped her hair. The humidity of August had turned it into something resembling a puff of cotton candy.

I achieved goal number one without any problem, thanks to Lola and Theo.

Clare pointed her toes and then flexed them, feeling a stretch up and down her calves.

Goal number two was harder. I came very close to making my swim in an hour, but I didn't exactly make it.

She sighed.

It didn't go like I planned, but I'm OK with that.

She kicked the sheets off her bed. The air was already so gluey and thick that she felt like she was being plunged into a pot of stew. She knew it would only get worse as the day went on.

All I've got left is goal number three.

"Mom! Grandma Lulu!" yelled Clare. She could hear them clattering around the kitchen. "Want to go fishing?"

...

"Where're we headed?" asked Bobb as he chugged away from the Burches' dock. He was the only Vogel free that day, and he'd offered to drive the boat for Clare, her mom, and Grandma Lulu.

"Definitely not the northeast corner of the lake," said Clare.

"Why not?" said Bobb.

She didn't hesitate. "Because it's much hotter now than it was in June, which means those shallow waters are too warm. The fish will be in deeper water. Deeper water is cooler, and it holds more oxygen, which the fish like."

Bobb nodded.

"How about the northwest corner?" she said.

"Works for me," said Bobb. "Some of my buddies have raised muskies there over the last couple weeks."

"They've 'raised muskies'?" said Grandma Lulu. "Good glory, what do you mean? They're taking care of them like little kids?"

"No, Grandma Lulu. It means you've gotten a musky's attention. Like, you've aroused its curiosity to the point where it's actually following your lure," said Clare.

"Oh. That's it?" Grandma Lulu looked disappointed.

"It's a big-time deal to raise a musky, Louise," said Bobb, solemnly. "I'd like to see your granddaughter get a follow one of these days."

"Me too," said Helen.

"Me three," said Clare. But she wanted more than a follow; she wanted an entire fish hooked to her Super Plopper.

"Why are muskies so impossible to catch?" said Grandma Lulu.

"Well, they aren't impossible, they're just super hard," said Clare. "They're at the top of the food chain. They don't have much to be afraid of, so they can be picky about what they eat. They like to check out a potential meal before they decide to take a bite."

"Even your dazzling Super Plopper?" said Grandma Lulu.

"Even my dazzling Super Plopper."

"Oh." Grandma Lulu frowned.

"*That*, Louise, is why muskies are called the fish of ten thousand casts." Bobb gunned the motor.

When they got to the deeper, cooler water, Grandma Lulu and Helen poked nightcrawlers onto their hooks. Grandma Lulu still muttered "Ew!" whenever she had to handle a worm, but Clare felt pride well up in her throat. *My grandmother hasn't just survived being up north, she's been totally amazing.*

Clare attached her Super Plopper to the end of her line. She took a deep breath and wriggled her shoulders to loosen them up. And then she began the process she'd practiced endlessly that summer. Cast, wait, reel, figure eight, repeat.

One hour became two.

"Hot as blazes, ain't it?" murmured Bobb while rubbing sunscreen into his ruddy cheeks.

Clare didn't stop. Cast, wait, reel, figure eight, repeat.

Her mom and Grandma Lulu caught a bunch of yellow perch that were big enough to keep for dinner. They placed them in a wire basket fastened to the outside of the boat, so that the perch would remain alive—and fresh—until they got to shore. Grandma Lulu planned out how they'd sauté the fish with butter, lemon, garlic, and fresh parsley.

"Geez, Louise, you're making me hungry," said Bobb.

But Clare didn't have time to think about food. Cast, wait, reel, figure eight, repeat.

Two hours became three.

Finally, Grandma Lulu set her rod along the bottom

of the boat and slumped against a cushion. Clare saw her eyes flutter behind her sunglasses. "It's official. I'm done fishing for the day. I'm going to melt, darlings."

"You're not going to melt, Mom," said Helen. "You're just spoiled from all the summers you've spent inside our air-conditioned house in Morrissey."

"Why didn't Anthony ever install air conditioning here at the cabin?" wailed Grandma Lulu.

"Because he was tough," said Helen.

From under her fishing hat, Grandma Lulu stuck out her tongue.

"Maybe the new owners can get air conditioning when they move in," said Clare. She tried to keep the sting out of her voice. Juliet had told them that a young couple was interested in making an offer on the cabin. According to her, it was an offer that Grandma Lulu couldn't refuse.

But Clare didn't want to think about Juliet. Cast, wait, reel, figure eight, repeat.

"Who needs air conditioning, anyway, when you can be out on a boat?" said Bobb.

"Do you really want me to answer that?" said Grandma Lulu.

Bobb guffawed.

Grandma Lulu sat up. "Maybe you can take me in to shore now? I need to sit in front of a fan and drink something very cold."

"One more cast?" asked Clare.

Grandma Lulu adjusted her sunglasses. "Have at it, darling."

Clare threw out her line. She counted to five, watching the swells she'd made in the water, and then reeled it back. She lowered the tip of her rod, and—

She was yanked forward by an impossible pressure at the end of her line.

She clamped her hands to the rod and took a step backward. She tried to regain her balance, but the force of whatever had chomped her Super Plopper was too strong. She lurched off the seat, tumbling to the bottom of the fishing boat and twisting her ankle. She yelped as stars burst in her eyes like roman candles, but she ignored them. She knew she needed to concentrate on one thing: not letting go of her rod.

"She's got a bite!" yelled Helen.

"And an injury, too! Oh, darling—" Grandma Lulu reached her hands under Clare's armpits and tried to help her up, but Clare was yanked forward again.

Bobb wrapped his arms around her waist to keep her from toppling over. His words in her ear were hushed and urgent. "You've hooked a musky, sweetheart. Hang on tight. You gotta put your whole body into this. I've got you."

Clare leaned back against him, and it relieved some of the mounting pain in her right ankle.

"It's dragging your line out!" yelled Helen.

Clare's reel buzzed like electricity through a power line.

"Use your muscles to pull it back. There you go! Steady, steady!" said Bobb.

Whatever was at the end of her line felt as solid as a tree trunk. Clare strained to pull it back through the churning, bubbling water. Her hands felt like they were breaking out in blisters. Her chest expanded with air. Inch by inch, she cranked her reel.

"It's fighting me!" she howled.

"Of course it is! Don't stop! Keep reeling! Keep pulling!" yelled Bobb.

Clare had never heard Bobb yell before.

"It's so close now, I can see it!" shrieked her mom.

"I can, too!" shrieked her grandmother.

"Helen, grab the net," said Bobb. "Louise, if you've got your cell phone—and I really hope you do—get it out. We're going to need the camera."

Clare's mom scrambled for the net. Grandma Lulu scrambled for her phone.

Without losing her footing on the seat or her grip on her rod, Clare peered over the side of the boat.

And there was her musky.

It was *way* bigger than the one that had followed Nedd's lure earlier that summer. It was silver, brown, and green, with vertical stripes along its body, and it thrashed angrily in the water.

Clare's arms and legs felt as if they were going to snap in half like kindling. Her ankle was starting to swell, but she didn't let go of her rod. She could hear the musky thwacking against the side of the boat.

"Helen, you and Louise have to net it. It's going to be real heavy," said Bobb. "Golly gee! Now that I can see it better . . . A musky that large is most definitely a female. They grow faster and bigger than the males."

Clare's mom and Grandma Lulu kneeled over the edge of the boat and maneuvered the net around the musky.

"Good glory, she's scarier than the bear was!" yelled Grandma Lulu. "Will she bite us?"

"She might. She's got sharp teeth, so don't get your hands near her mouth," said Bobb.

"I can't really see her teeth. All I can see is the Super Plopper. It looks like it's stuck in her lip," said Helen.

"Good, that's good," said Bobb. "I'm glad she didn't swallow it. That's when things can get messy."

The pressure on Clare's rod let up a little bit. She could feel the fish starting to tire.

"She's in!" yelled her mom. "She's in the net!"

"Keep the net slightly in the water so she can breathe. I'm sure she's feeling panicked." Bobb eased Clare down to the seat. "I need to dislodge the hook now, sweetheart." He opened his tackle box and seized a set of large needle-nose pliers. While Clare tried to settle her quivering limbs, he bent over the side of the boat.

"You're not hurting her, are you?" Clare rubbed her clammy knees. "You're not hurting the musky?"

"No," said Bobb. "She's stunned, but that's to be expected. I almost can't believe my eyes, Clare. You've caught a dandy! Can you try to stand up? As soon as I get the hook out, I'll hold her up. You'll need to stand close, right next to me. Louise, you take the picture, OK? Helen, get the soft measuring tape from my tackle box. This'll go fast, so get ready!"

In one ballet-like motion, Bobb stood and turned to Clare. He was grasping the musky under her jaw. He placed his other hand under her flank so he could hold her horizontally. "*Now*," he said to Clare.

She wedged herself between Bobb and the fish.

Grandma Lulu held up her phone and started snapping pictures.

Clare's mom burst into tears.

Clare looked at the fish—the fish she'd worked so hard for, the fish that had eluded her grandfather his whole life. She placed her hand on the musky's firm, slimy body and looked into her eyes, which were round, black, and fathomless. The musky looked back at her, and Clare felt a thrill of understanding. The fish seemed to be saying, *You did it. You worked me hard. You put up a good fight.*

Clare leaned closer to the musky and whispered, "Thanks. You put up a good fight, too."

"Helen, can you measure her quick?" said Bobb. "We gotta get her back in the water."

"We aren't keeping her?" yelled Grandma Lulu.

Laura Anne Bird

"Heck, no," said Bobb. "You don't eat musky."

Helen stretched the measuring tape along the musky's body and then around her belly like a belt. "Forty-eight inches long. And twenty-two inches thick," she announced, as her tears morphed into hiccups.

"Gracious sakes! Clare Burch, you've just caught Alwyn's biggest musky of the year!" shouted Bobb. "She's at least thirty pounds, by the feel of her."

"I did it," said Clare. "I just caught a musky in the musky capital of the world."

"A *gigantic* musky," said Bobb. "Should we turn her loose now?"

Clare nodded. "You belong back in the lake," she murmured to the fish.

They leaned over the side of the boat, which tipped slightly under their combined weight. Bobb carefully slipped the fish underwater but didn't release his grip. "We'll keep her here a second or two, so she can revive herself."

Sure enough, being back in the lake appeared to give the musky a jolt of energy.

It's like watching Mom and Grandma Lulu take their first sips of coffee in the morning, thought Clare.

The musky whipped her tail right out of Bobb's hand and gave it a furious shake. Bobb released his grip, and Clare watched her musky disappear, leaving nothing behind but a wrinkle in the water.

She released all the oxygen she'd been holding in her lungs and glanced around the boat. She felt like she was returning to Earth after visiting a different galaxy. Everyone was soaked with sweat, lake water, tears, and snot—and her ankle was turning as green as the musky's scales had been. But none of it bothered her.

"I accomplished goal number three!" she bellowed.

Bobb helped her sit down in the boat. Clare could feel his hands shaking. He took off his fishing hat and ran a hand through his damp hair.

Helen was still sniffling, trying to wipe her tears away with one of the boat cushions.

Grandma Lulu looked bewildered. Her sunglasses and fishing hat were askew. "If we can't actually eat a musky, *then why in the world have you been trying to catch one all summer?*" She threw her hands in the air.

Clare grinned. "*Why?* For the challenge! For the hard work and exercise! For the agony and the triumph and the peace!"

You were right, Henry David Thoreau.

"Amen," said Bobb. His voice sounded sticky with emotion.

"I did it for me, and I did it for Grandpa Anthony," said Clare. "He told me to make it a great year and a great life, and that's exactly what I'm doing."

Thirty
The Mobbing

After being housebound for a couple of days so she could elevate her puffy ankle, Clare was back on the water.

"Are you sure you're OK to paddle?" asked Lola from the front of the canoe.

"Oh my gosh, yes," said Clare from the back. "I couldn't stay inside for another minute. My mom wrapped up my ankle super tight. It's fine." She wriggled her toes in contentment.

"Only if you're positive," said Theo. He was in the middle of the canoe, with Roger snoring in his lap.

"I'm positive," said Clare. "And you're all right holding Roger?"

"Yep," said Theo. "It was my idea to bring him along, anyway."

"Just when you think you've seen it all," said Lola, shaking her head. "A wiener dog wearing a life jacket."

"Grandma Lulu bought it for him," said Clare.

Theo patted Roger's head. "You look good in orange, little buddy."

"Where to, Lo?" Clare didn't care where they went, she was just thrilled to be smelling the rich lake water and feeling the waves gently lift and lower the canoe.

"Let's go out to the isthmus. Maybe we'll see the mama otter and her babies again."

Clare used her paddle to turn the canoe toward the isthmus. "Onward."

As they skimmed across the water, they chatted about Clare's musky, and Musky Days, and Helen's paintings, which were almost ready to be hung at the makeshift gallery.

"I bet a ton of people will come to the show," said Lola. "My mom's been sending out press releases and calling reporters."

"I hope it's packed. Between your mom and my mom, they've been working so hard to get everything ready," said Clare.

When they arrived at the isthmus, Lola climbed out and sloshed through the shallow water. She set down her paddle and pulled the canoe onto the grass. "Do you guys want to get out for a couple minutes? We could let Roger sniff around."

"Sure," said Clare. "It'll feel good to stretch my legs."

Lola helped Clare climb out, and then she lent a hand to Theo and Roger, whose tail was already flicking back and forth. He started to nose around the grass.

"He definitely smells something," said Theo. "What do you think it is?"

"He's never been on the isthmus before," said Clare. "Frogs, snakes, turtles. Who knows?"

"I was hoping the otters would be here," said Lola. She made a pouty face.

Clare, Lola, and Theo watched Roger as he explored, and they kept him from getting too close to the water's edge. As they poked around the isthmus for signs of wildlife, their life jackets glowed dazzlingly in the sun.

"I bet your mom would love to paint a picture of us right now," said Lola.

"We'd make good subjects," said Theo, "and the light is just how she likes it."

"Bright," said Clare.

The light was so bright, in fact, that none of them noticed the dinghy on Lake Lyons, moving toward them.

"Well, look who's here," yelled Jack across the water. "If it ain't City Girl and her little squad. Why're you limping so bad? Is it because of that musky you supposedly caught?"

Clare closed her eyes. She tried to picture the plaque at the library—and Jack's hopeless little face in the photograph.

"I heard all about that dandy," continued Jack. "But it's impossible to imagine *you* catching it. You're such a shrimp that your hands probably don't even make it around the rod. I'm sure it was Bobb Vogel who reeled it in and then gave you all the credit."

Roger barked.

"Leave us alone. We're not bothering you at all," said Lola.

A crow in the sky cawed and swooped down into one of the trees on the isthmus.

"You bother me just by being here," said Jack.

"Well, what're you going to do about it?" yelled Lola. "If we bother you so much, then go away. No one's forcing you to follow us around."

Now there was a second crow in the sky. It cawed and joined the first crow on the branch, and they started squawking like old friends.

"Just ignore him," said Clare. "Pretend he's not here." *Although that's probably what everyone does, which doesn't help him at all.*

A third crow landed on the branch and joined in the screeching.

"Dumb crows. I can't even hear myself think!" Jack reached down into his boat. When he stood up on the seat, he was holding a BB gun. "Shut up, will ya?" He pointed the BB gun away from the isthmus and fired in the air.

Roger howled.

Lola screamed.

"He's nuts," said Theo.

Clare pressed her palms to her cheeks, which were pulsing hotly along with her ankle. The crows were shrieking louder now as a fourth—and a fifth, sixth, seventh—joined them.

"What is *happening*?" said Lola.

"Oh my gosh, I think they're mobbing," said Clare. She'd learned about mobbing when she'd done her report for school, but she'd never seen it happen in real life.

An eighth, ninth, tenth, eleventh, twelfth, and thirteenth crow landed in the tree. But then Clare lost count, because the branches were covered.

"It's true! They're really mobbing!" She remembered that crows gathered in big groups to harass and scare off predators, but they also did it to protect their babies. *Are they mobbing to protect US?* She shook her head, feeling muddled and unsure.

But then again, why would that be so weird? I'm not Saint Kevin or anything, but I've always cared about nature and animals. Maybe it's good karma coming back to me.

"That is so cool," said Theo, looking up at the crows, but Clare could barely make out his words.

Jack, meanwhile, was trying to cover his ears. His face seemed to crumple in rage, and he raised his BB gun again.

"No!" yelled Clare. It felt like slow motion as Jack pointed the BB gun at the trees right above her.

He pulled the trigger. The *pop* of the BB gun made Clare jump, but the crows didn't seem to be disturbed. A few flapped their wings and rearranged themselves, but that was it.

"I think he's too far away to hit anything," said Theo.

Jack pulled the trigger again.

"We have to get out of here," said Clare, as the crows carried on. "This is crazy." But as she leaned down to scoop up Roger, the isthmus seemed to tilt under her feet. Apparently, Jack was too far away to hit a crow—but he wasn't too far away to hit a dog. One of the BBs had struck Roger.

He was on his side, whimpering. Blood was flowing from his thigh. Clare made a noise that sounded like a crying animal—or maybe it was Roger himself. She couldn't tell. The inside of her head felt like it was lined with wool. *I have to think clearly. I have to do something*.

Immediately, Lola and Theo were at her side, like bookends that would keep her from tipping over. None of them had their cell phones.

Clare lifted Roger and held him close. His doggy life jacket was smeared and dirty. She whispered a string of words into his ear. "It's OK. It's OK, sweet Roger. I've got you. I won't let you go. Please buddy, you have to be all right."

Clare told Theo to take off his t-shirt. He jerked it over his head and handed it to her. She pressed it against Roger's thigh to staunch the bleeding.

"It's all my fault," he cried. "I begged you to bring him along!"

"No, it's *my* fault," said Lola. "I wanted to paddle to the isthmus!"

Clare shook her head *no* at them. *There's no time for guilt or blame.*

"Whistle!" she yelled at Lola. "Do your whistle!"

Lola stuck her fingers in her mouth. She ran back and forth on the isthmus, sending her shrill call for help out to Lake Alwyn and Lake Lyons.

"We have to go. We have to paddle back and get help for Roger," Clare said to Theo.

His tortoiseshell glasses had slipped down his sweaty nose. "Give Roger to me."

Clare handed Roger and the t-shirt to Theo. "Look what you've done!" she screamed at Jack. Every bit of her patience was gone. "You've killed my dog!"

Jack was motionless, his BB gun still raised in the air.

"Who do you think you are?" Clare clenched her fists, but she was distracted by one of the crows, which had dived from the tree and was sailing effortlessly out to the rowboat. His black wings looked ghoulish as he flew straight for Jack.

With a look of horror on his face, Jack lifted his hands

to cover his head, dropping his BB gun at the same time. It clanked against the side of the boat and plopped into the lake.

The crow circled Jack, who was wobbling in the boat, and flew back to the tree.

It's over, thought Clare. *Go away, now, Jack, so that Lola, Theo, and I can get out of here with poor, bleeding Roger.*

Jack seemed to snap back to attention. He squinted at his empty hand.

"It fell in the lake!" yelled Clare. "Serves you right."

But then Jack started to tip, first to the right, then to the left, his arms circling. His feet flew up from under him as if he'd stepped on a banana peel. It would have been funny like a dumb TV show, but it wasn't—because just like his BB gun, Jack hit the side of the boat and toppled into the water.

Clare blinked in disbelief. She stared at the lake, willing Jack to emerge.

"It looked like he really clocked his head," said Lola.

"Oh no," said Theo. His glasses had slipped so far down his nose that they fell right off.

Lola reached down to grab them, and she shoved them back on his face.

The crows stopped cawing. Clare could feel their eyes on her, as if they were wondering what she would do next.

Hurry, hurry, hurry.

"I'm going in." She kicked off her flip-flops, tore off her life jacket, and ran into the water. Her ankle throbbed as she made her way through the rocks and weeds. She would've given anything to have a starting block or a raft to dive from—*anything* to keep her from losing precious seconds. As soon as it was deep enough, she hurled her body into a front crawl. She kept her face forward, above the water, hoping that Jack's head would pop up and this all would be a horrible joke.

Her hair had come loose from her ponytail and was fastened to her cheeks and eyes like wet cords. It made it so much harder to see. *My swim cap,* she thought with longing. *My goggles.* But she kept her gaze on the spot where Jack had gone in.

Lola continued her whistling on the isthmus.

Clare made it to Jack's spot. But the rowboat had drifted, so she wasn't sure if she was in the right place. "I'm here, Jack, I'm here," she shouted.

She took a breath. Below the surface, the lake had a churchy hush. Lola's whistling was replaced by the sound of a thousand rising bubbles. *Are they coming from me or Jack?* She couldn't tell.

The water was a murky green. It wasn't easy to see, but she could just make out Jack's fingertips, which were undulating below her like minnows. He was only a couple feet away. She tried to swim toward him, but her lungs ached. She rose to the surface to take a breath.

She dived again and pushed her body downward, hard, fast and straight like a missile. Her fingertips brushed against Jack's. She grabbed onto them and pulled. He felt surprisingly light as his body moved toward hers. She tried to shift her fingers to his wrist so she could maintain a better hold, but he started to slip from her grasp.

No! Don't let go! She heard her own voice shouting in her head. *Mrs. Wilson, I'll do anything to save your son. It may have been Grandpa Anthony's time to go, but it's not Jack's.*

Clare grabbed at Jack's wrist again and clenched as hard as she could. She kicked, and together they rose up toward the light of day.

Her head emerged above the water first, then his, lolling like an overcooked noodle. She gasped and coughed and stretched one of her arms around Jack's chest. She needed to keep him—and her own self—afloat.

Before exhaustion and a sense of dread could overtake her, Clare felt hands under her own armpits.

Lola and Theo had paddled out to her in the canoe. Lola was reaching down and holding her up. "Don't let go of Jack. I won't let go of you."

Theo was in the back of the canoe. He was still holding Roger.

Clare started to tread water. Her bandage had come loose, and it was trailing from her ankle and tickling her leg. Her ankle ached, but she knew she couldn't focus on that.

"The whistling worked," said Lola. "There's a boat on its way to us right now. Hang on just a minute longer."

"Roger?" whispered Clare. She could hear the roar of a motorboat speeding toward them. She closed her eyes and wanted nothing more than to weep right into Jack's skull.

"Roger's breathing," said Theo. "Is . . . Jack?"

Clare tried to get a better look at Jack's face, but it was difficult from behind. She could tell he was as white as Grandma Lulu's fancy bedsheets, and he was sporting a lump on his temple that made her flinch. She shook him just enough so his head wouldn't slide underwater. "Jack," she said. "Come on, Jack, wake up."

Clare imagined Abby pummeling one of the boxing bags at her gym. She screwed her hand into a fist and jabbed Jack's back as hard as she could. She had to get the water out of his lungs.

She heard a wheeze inside his body. She hit him again, harder.

Jack made a warbling sound and let out a weak, wet-sounding cough.

Clare was getting ready to whack him a third time, but he groaned.

"He's alive!" she said. "But I'm so tired. I can't do this for much longer."

"If anyone can do it, it's you," yelled Lola. "And the motorboat's almost here!"

Clare heard the flapping of wings as the crows flew off and away from the isthmus. Waves surged toward her as the motorboat got closer.

If anyone can do this, it's me. She repeated it in her head, until she heard shouting from the motorboat.

"We called nine-one-one!" the people onboard yelled. "We need to get you guys to the public dock." They pulled Clare and Jack from the water, and they helped Lola, Theo, and Roger out of the canoe.

Clare felt herself being wrapped in a towel. She closed her eyes and heard the gunning of the motor. She had so many questions. *Is everyone all right? Is Jack going to be OK? Who has Roger?* But she shoved the questions aside. All she could do was focus on her breathing. In and out. In and out.

She trusted that her inhales and exhales—along with the motorboat, which was tearing across Lake Lyons— would get her safely to shore.

Thirty-One
The Conversation

"Why haven't they let me go yet?" Clare stared furiously out the hospital window. "I can't believe just a few hours ago I was paddling in the canoe, and now I'm stuck here. I want to go home. I don't like hospitals. I feel fine. I just want to see Roger."

"They want to make sure, one last time, that your vital signs and ankle look good," said her mom.

"Roger's not at the cabin, anyway. He's at the animal hospital, remember, darling?" said Grandma Lulu.

Images floated through Clare's head, but they didn't seem to be in the right order. "I guess. It's all sort of fuzzy."

"That's to be expected." Helen rubbed Clare's arm.

"You've been through a lot." Grandma Lulu rubbed Clare's other arm.

"But Roger's fine, right?" Clare couldn't stop thinking about her juddering, bloody dog. She wanted to throw up.

"The vet called a little while ago. She said Roger's just got a flesh wound," said her mom. "The BB grazed his thigh, that's all. His life jacket was protecting his little belly."

"And you girls teased me for buying it," said Grandma Lulu, making a *tsk* sound.

"Everything could've been so much worse," said Clare's mom. "All that matters is that you're OK, and that you saved that boy from drowning—even though he put you kids in a very bad situation."

Clare knew her mom was right. Somehow, she, Lola, Theo, Roger, and even Jack were all in one piece. She remembered how the motorboat had practically *flown* across Lake Lyons. The people onboard had made sure Jack was breathing. They'd applied a clean towel to Roger's injury. And they'd kept Clare from pitching over in a slump.

When the ambulance met them at the public dock, Clare couldn't believe how unburdened she felt as the paramedics lifted her out of the boat. While she'd been in the water with Jack, he'd been heavy as a grand piano against her body; his legs kept getting in the way of hers, and his hair had been in her mouth. Now, it was just her, free in her own skin again.

The paramedics wheeled Clare and Jack into the ambulance on stretchers. *How funny*, she thought. *I didn't even have to fight my way in this time.*

She clamped her eyes shut against the red-and-blue lights and tried to ignore the scream of the siren. She wasn't prepared for the wave of memories it stirred up in her, and she had to remind herself that it wasn't New Year's Eve. *This time is totally different. Grandpa Anthony didn't have a chance, but Jack does.*

As the paramedics poked and prodded her, Clare realized how wet her clothes were. They made her skin feel gritty and gross. The bandage on her ankle had vanished, and she guessed it had sunk to the bottom of Lake Lyons.

"My mom?" said Clare to one of the paramedics. "My grandmother?"

"They're on their way to the hospital. You'll see 'em real soon, kiddo," the paramedic replied.

And when she did, they'd nearly suffocated each other with their hugs.

"Knock, knock!" A nurse tapped on the door of Clare's hospital room.

"May I please leave now?" said Clare.

"Not yet, but I like your tenacity." The nurse chuckled. "You've got a visitor."

Before Clare could ask who was visiting her, the nurse pushed Jack in. He was sitting in a wheelchair, and a bandage was wrapped around his head.

"You look terrible," said Clare, trying not to gawk. *Oh my gosh, I can't believe I just said that.* "But . . . I'm glad to see you." She shoved her hands under the blanket so he wouldn't notice the tremor in them.

Her mom and grandmother looked at Jack with wary expressions.

"It's OK, you guys," said Clare.

Helen frowned. "But . . ."

"Can you just give me and Jack a few minutes?" said Clare.

"Are you sure?" asked her mom.

Clare nodded.

"Let's go to the cafeteria and get some coffee, darling," said Grandma Lulu. She took Helen's hand and blew a kiss at Clare.

They'd barely left the room when Jack began to cry. "I'm so sorry I've been so horrible this summer. I'm sorry I followed you guys around and said awful things and shot BBs and killed your dog—"

"—Jack, wait—"

"The truth is that I have *horrible* aim. Like, I'm *terrible* with slingshots and BB guns and hunting rifles and *everything*. My dad makes me do all that stuff, though, because he says I'm from the Northwoods, and that's what guys are supposed to do. But I hate it all. I don't even like to *swim*, which is why I have to wear a stupid inner tube every time I get in the lake."

By now, Jack had rivulets of snot trickling from his nostrils. Clare grabbed the box of tissues next to her bed and tossed it to him.

"How is it that someone who can't shoot *anything* manages to murder an innocent dog when he wasn't even *trying*?" Jack went on, wiping his nose. "I was bored, and I was feeling crappy, and that's no excuse, but—"

"Jack!" said Clare. "My dog isn't dead. He's *alive*. The BB just grazed his thigh."

Jack stared at Clare.

"Roger's *fine*," she said. "You are, too . . . Right?"

"Yeah, sure." He shook his head ruefully. "But only because of you. I would've drowned if you hadn't come in after me."

"Well, I don't know about that . . ." But she *did* know. She had rescued him, and it'd been grueling and scary, but she'd do it again in a heartbeat.

He blew his nose, making a noise that reminded Clare of a tropical bird. "I mean, seriously—how do you thank someone for saving your life?" he said.

"It's OK. You don't have to thank me or say anything else."

Jack blew his nose again.

Then Clare said, "I'm really sorry about your mom."

He made a puzzled expression. "How'd you know about her?"

"I saw the plaque at the library."

He scrunched his face up. "She died last year. Three-hundred-seventy-four days ago, to be exact, but who's counting? Breast cancer. She left me and my dad behind. He owns Dutch's, the restaurant just off Main Street. You can smell the onion rings a mile away."

Clare nodded. She loved those onion rings.

"He works all the time now. I think he's in denial or something. And then he comes home reeking like French fries. I don't have any brothers or sisters, so I'm alone a lot."

"That sounds awful," said Clare. "I lost somebody, too."

Jack looked down into his lap. "I know. I'm sorry I brought up your grandfather the day I came out to your raft. That was mean. I wasn't thinking straight."

"Don't you have anybody to hang out with? Or anything to cheer you up?" Clare thought about all the lifeboats that had saved her that year: books, swimming, nature, friends, her family. The urn. "I mean, it's OK to be sad, but I think it helps to have something else to focus on."

Jack shrugged. "I guess I'll have to figure that out."

"Knock, knock!" The nurse had returned.

"Do I actually have to go home in this thing?" said Jack, gesturing to the wheelchair.

"Not as long as you don't feel like fainting or anything. We'll make sure you can stand on your own two

Laura Anne Bird

feet before you're released," said the nurse. "Ready to go back to your room?"

Jack smiled at Clare. Clare smiled back.

"Ready as I'll ever be," he said.

Clare felt sorry to see him go. He was like a shadowy, solitary character in a novel that she wanted to keep reading. "Hang in there, OK?" The words felt flimsy, but she didn't know what else to say.

The nurse started to turn Jack's wheelchair around, but he put out his arm to stop her. "Hey! Wait!" He turned back to Clare. "I wanted to tell you that your musky was *epic*."

"My musky?" Clare gaped. "How'd you see it?"

"The pictures of it have gone viral, don'tcha know? The Vogel brothers have posted it all over social media. Everyone in Alwyn is talking about it. I'm not into fishing, but you should hear my dad and the other guys at Dutch's. They're so jealous."

"The Vogel brothers are on *social media*?" was all Clare managed to say.

"I bet you'll be crowned Mister Musky."

"No way," she said. "You're nuts."

"Tell me something I don't already know."

Clare grinned. *He's not so bad. He's actually pretty funny.*

"Guess I'll see you around." Jack waved as the nurse pushed him out of the room. "Thanks again for saving my life."

214

"Anytime," Clare called out.

Then she added, "I mean it," even though he was already gone.

Thirty-Two
The Calls

Clare's cell phone buzzed first thing the next day.

"Just a few more minutes of sleep," she murmured into her pillow.

The phone buzzed again, and she forced herself to sit up.

Clare didn't recognize the number on the screen. *Maybe it's Jack*, she thought, then felt silly. *I'll probably never see or hear from him again. I mean, why would I?*

"Hello?" Clare's voice was creaky. She cleared her throat.

"Do I have the pleasure of speaking with Clare Burch?" said the voice on the other end.

"Yes." She rubbed her eyes and stifled a yawn. "This is Clare Burch."

"This is Mayor Betty Sue Bindlebauer."

Who is Mayor Betty Sue Bindlebauer? Clare yawned again.

"This is Betty Sue Bindlebauer," the voice repeated, "the mayor of Alwyn."

Clare's mouth fell open. Why would the mayor of Alwyn be calling her? How did the mayor of Alwyn even know who she was? "Um, hi?"

Mayor Bindlebauer congratulated Clare on her musky. "We're sure proud of you for catching that dandy! It's the biggest that anyone's hooked this summer."

"Oh," said Clare. "Thanks."

"Which means," continued Mayor Bindlebauer, "that my city council and I have unanimously chosen you to be this year's Mister Musky!"

Clare pulled the cell phone away from her ear and stared at it.

"I must admit, we've never done *anything* like this before," Mayor Bindlebauer was saying as Clare stuck the phone back to her ear.

"Done what?" asked Clare.

"Usually Mister Musky is an older, retired gentleman. We've never had a teenager, and we've certainly never had a girl."

"Oh," said Clare.

"But I couldn't be more excited. Not only is it well-deserved on your part, but I'm simply thrilled about you breaking our glass ceiling."

"Glass ceiling . . . ?"

"Our Musky Days parade is next week, as you probably already know," the mayor went on. "You'll be crowned in a ceremony right before the parade begins, in the parking lot of Bobb's Bait Shop. Be there bright and early. You'll sit in a convertible at the front of the procession, and we'll give you lots of candy to toss out along the route."

By now, Clare's grogginess had vanished, and her heart was pounding. *Me? Mister Musky? Sitting in a convertible at the head of the parade? Tossing out candy?*

"Does this sound good?" asked Mayor Bindlebauer. "Are you game?"

"Yes," said Clare. "I'm totally game."

When she hung up with Mayor Bindlebauer, Clare flopped back onto her bed and dissolved into laughter.

I never in a million years expected this, she thought, wiping away the tears that had pooled beneath her eyelashes.

Her cell phone buzzed again. It was a different number.

"Hello?" said Clare.

"Is this Clare?" The girl's voice sounded familiar, but Clare couldn't recall where she'd heard it before.

"Yes, this is Clare."

"My name is Lucy, and I'm calling from the Al-Skis Water Ski Club."

It was one of the announcers from the show Clare had gone to on her birthday!

"Oh," said Clare, "hi." *Why is Lucy from the Al-Skis calling me?*

"I just heard from Mayor Bindlebauer that you accepted the city council's invitation to be crowned as this year's Mister Musky."

"Wow," said Clare. "News sure travels fast around here."

"Every August, we end our Al-Skis season by asking the new Mister Musky if he—or . . . she?—would be a guest skier in our final show."

Clare closed her eyes and pictured the tall pyramid of water skiers. On top was the littlest one, gleefully waving the Al-Skis flag.

"But Mister Musky always says no, because he's retired and no fun at all—and because he doesn't want to get up in front of the crowd wearing a swimsuit."

"Oh," said Clare.

"So," continued Lucy, "would you be the first Mister Musky *ever* to ski in our last show of the summer?"

Clare opened her mouth, but nothing came out. She remembered how fast the Al-Skis boats had whizzed by, and how strong the skiers were, climbing up on each other like it was no big deal.

"Please?" said Lucy. "It would be great to have you on our team."

"But I don't know how to water ski," said Clare.

"We'll teach you everything you need to know," said Lucy.

Clare's first instinct was to toss down her phone and run into the great room. She'd stand next to the fireplace and whisper frantically to the urn, weighing all the pros and cons of accepting Lucy's invitation. But she reminded herself that in a matter of days, the urn would be empty.

Clare could easily imagine what Grandpa Anthony would say if he were still alive. She knew he'd be her biggest cheerleader. *But he's not alive. He can't cheer me on or help me figure out what to do. That's my job now.*

She jiggled her nearly healed ankle and knew that it would hold up just fine. So would the rest of her body.

"Yes," said Clare. "I would love to be in your last show of the summer."

Lucy shrieked. "It's a date, then!" She said the show was set for the following week, after Musky Days was over, and she listed off the practices that Clare would need to attend.

Clare was glad everything would fit into her schedule before leaving for Morrissey. After hanging up with Lucy, she fired off a text to Emmy and Olive to share her news, and then one to Lola and Theo. She giggled as their happy responses and funny emojis flew back and forth. She hoped her phone wouldn't blow up.

Clare heard her mom and Grandma Lulu making espresso in the kitchen, so she hopped out of bed. She ran out of her room and curtsied flamboyantly in front of them. "Hello, Mom. Hello, Grandma Lulu. Did you know that you're living under the very same roof as this year's Mister—"

But she was interrupted by the ringing of a phone. This time it was Grandma Lulu's.

Grandma Lulu looked at the screen and glanced at Helen.

"Go on and get it." Clare's mom frowned.

"Good morning, Juliet," said Grandma Lulu into her cell.

"What were you saying, Clare?" said Helen, distractedly. "About living under the same roof as . . . ?"

But Clare wasn't thinking about Mister Musky anymore. She was listening to her grandmother, who'd left the kitchen and was pacing around the cabin.

"That's wonderful news," Grandma Lulu said to Juliet, but her voice sounded anything but happy. "It's an offer we can't refuse."

Clare pulled herself up from her curtsy before she could tumble to the ground.

Thirty-Three
The Emptying

Clare sat down on one of the chairs on the dock. She scooted to the side so there was enough room for the urn, too. The setting sun slanted across the lake, bringing a golden softness to the light.

Clare rubbed the smooth wood and thought about the Tilt-A-Whirl of experiences and emotions she'd been on that summer. *I still feel like play dough, but I've gotten used to being smooshed down and stretched apart. I know I won't rip in half,* she thought. *I'm glad I could come to Alwyn to figure that out.*

Behind her, Clare heard her mom and Grandma Lulu push open the cabin door and move toward her on the dock.

"Thank you for being here all this time, Grandpa Anthony," she whispered to the urn. "I've loved having you around a little longer."

"Darling?" Grandma Lulu rested her hand on Clare's back.

"Ready?" said Clare's mom.

"Ready as I'll ever be." Clare clasped the urn to her chest and climbed into the fishing boat. They chugged out onto the lake, and after a few minutes, Clare pointed. "There." It was the northwest corner, where she'd caught her musky.

When they reached Clare's chosen spot, Helen turned off the motor. They were quiet for a few minutes, rolling in the gentle waves of early evening.

Clare unfastened the silver latch and opened the box. She removed the thick plastic bag that was inside. It was dense and lumpy.

"I'm glad there's no wind tonight," said her mom.

"As much as we love him, we certainly don't need Anthony blowing in our faces." Grandma Lulu squeezed Clare's shoulder.

Clare unzipped the bag. She reached in and felt the ashes against her fingers. They were pebbly and dry, like the sand that had filled her sandbox as a kid. She cupped some in her palm and stood up.

She lifted her hand carefully in an underhand pitch and flung the ashes away from the boat. Some seemed to dissipate in the air, while others fell heavily onto the surface of the water and were absorbed immediately.

It's like the lake has been waiting for Grandpa Anthony all along.

Clare passed the bag around the boat, and they took turns scattering the ashes until they were gone. There were no speeches or tears, just the sounds of animals calling from the air, the water, and the land. Clare knew that her grandfather wouldn't have wanted it any other way.

After they finished, Clare's mom pointed the boat back toward shore. "Dad's headstone is finally ready," she said. "We can have it installed at the cemetery before we go back to Morrissey."

Clare imagined his marker being placed right next to the kids', and she smiled to herself. "That means we've done everything he wanted."

"Our to-do list is complete," said Helen.

Clare held the empty urn as they boated back to the dock. She couldn't believe how light it felt.

Thirty-Four
The Change of Plans: Part II

As Clare's mom tied the boat to the dock, Grandma Lulu played with one of her curls. *Boing. Boing. Boing.* "There's something I need to tell you girls," she said.

"I already know what it is." Clare sighed. *Just get it out in the open so I can move on.*

"Well, you know that Juliet called yesterday to tell me there was an offer on the cabin. It's that young couple, with two children."

"That's nice," said Helen, smiling wistfully. "I like that little kids will be able to grow up here."

"I hope they love the raft as much as I do," said Clare. "We could leave them the fishing boat and the canoe, too."

"What a sweet idea, darling," said Grandma Lulu, "but I don't think so."

Clare turned to Grandma Lulu. "Why not?"

"Mom, we'll never use that stuff in Morrissey," said Helen. "Let's be practical."

"We're not leaving them anything," said Grandma Lulu, "because we're not selling the cabin."

Clare almost dropped the urn. "What?"

"If they're not buying the cabin, then who is?" said Helen, looking alarmed. "Please don't tell me we have to start the process with Juliet all over again."

"I've spent thirty years not coming up north," said Grandma Lulu. "Why did I stay in Morrissey when I could've been here, with you girls? It makes me sad to think about all the hummingbirds and snapping turtles and meat raffles and campfires I've missed."

"Bears, too?" added Clare.

"I wouldn't go *that* far, darling," said Grandma Lulu. "What about the Vogels and the Porters? They've become our family. And now Anthony's here, too." She gestured toward the lake. "I can't believe I'm admitting it, but I've come to adore Alwyn. We can't say goodbye to it forever, don't you agree?"

"Of course I agree," said Helen. "I never wanted to sell the cabin in the first place. Why didn't we have this discussion earlier?"

"Because it's taken me the whole summer to understand a few things," said Grandma Lulu.

Clare understood perfectly. "But . . . how can we afford to keep it?"

"We'll make it work," said Grandma Lulu with a clap of her hands. "Starting with me kicking off my brand-new career."

"But that doesn't make sense," said Clare. "You told me it would be too hard to keep the cabin if you had a job."

"It's funny how things work out, isn't it?" Grandma Lulu gave a sly grin. "Turns out, my new career is going to be in Morrissey . . . *and* in Alwyn. Marisa and I are starting a company."

"What?" said Clare.

Helen's mouth fell open.

"It's been such fun for me to watch Marisa coordinate all the plans for your art show, Helen. I love how your creativity and her good business sense have come together so synergistically. Because of your partnership, the show will be a whopping success—I just know it."

"But what does that have to do with you, Grandma Lulu?" said Clare. *And what does 'synergistically' mean?*

"In college, I studied the same things as Marisa did. We both have business degrees, and I have a lot of the same skills as her—I just need to put them to use. I'll learn whatever else I need to know."

"But what will you and Marisa be *doing*?" said Clare.

"We're creating an artist residency! We're going to take the second floor of the building she rented for Helen's show and turn it into an apartment and studio for artists who want a quiet place to work for a while. Then they can show off their pieces in the gallery when they're done."

Clare could totally envision it. "Think of all the artists living in big cities who will want the chance to come up north. They'll be able to get in touch with all their senses here. They'll find their creativity, just like you, Mom."

Helen gave a quick nod of her head before asking, "But where will you *be*, Mom? I don't get it."

"I'll be in Morrissey, and Marisa will be here in Alwyn," said Grandma Lulu. "But it'll be easy for us to stay connected because, believe it or not, I've got that technology thing nailed down now. There'll be times when I need to come up north, but that shouldn't be a problem, because I'll just stay here at the cabin. I've been talking with the Vogel brothers about the upkeep, and they'll do anything to help."

"Can I come with you?" said Clare. "Like when I don't have school? Then I can see Lola and Theo and the Vogels." *And maybe even Jack.*

"Of course. You're my road trip partner," said Grandma Lulu. "We'll stop and get frozen custard every single time," she added in a whisper.

Helen shifted from one foot to another. "This is a lot to process all at once, but I guess I've got some news of my own to share." She raised her palms awkwardly.

"What is it?" Clare's head was spinning like the reel of her musky rod.

"You know how much I love teaching in Morrissey, but I've been thinking about making a change. I'd love to see more of the world, like I should've done when I was younger, so last month, on a whim, I applied to an international art teacher exchange program. I'm really sorry I didn't mention it to you guys. I just didn't want to get my hopes up."

"And?" said Grandma Lulu.

"I just found out that I was . . . accepted."

"Mom!" yelled Clare. "That's awesome."

"But there's a problem." Helen's expression was forlorn.

"What's the problem?" said Clare.

"It's in Paris," said Helen.

"Paris, *France*?" said Clare.

"You've always wanted to go to Paris, France!" said Grandma Lulu. "Or maybe that was just me," she added under her breath.

"If I accepted the offer, I'd be gone for the entire second semester of the school year. I'd be leaving the two of you in Morrissey, without me," said Clare's mom.

"OK," said Clare, slowly.

How is this all going to work? she started to wonder—but she already knew the answer. *It might take a little while, but I'll adjust. Grandma Lulu and I will be fine. We'll take good care of each other, even if the house is a lot messier without the taskmaster in charge. Plus,*

229

look at how happy my mom is after just two months up north. I can only imagine what an entire semester in Europe will do for her!

"The program sounds amazing, Mom. You can't turn it down," said Clare.

"When the universe asks you to do something difficult, you have to listen up and do it," said Grandma Lulu.

"It'll be a bigger salary for me, which means I can help cover expenses for the cabin," said Helen.

"It's settled then," said Grandma Lulu. "I can't wait to call Juliet and tell her I'm tearing up the papers!"

Clare tried to draw her mom and grandmother together in a hug, but the urn, still tucked under her arm, knocked right into them.

She set it down on the dock and tried again.

Pulling her little family close, Clare thought of her grandfather.

He'd been their compass for so long.

But look at us now, she marveled.

We're each pointing in our very own direction.

Thirty-Five
The Brand-New Chapter

Clare stood in front of one of her mom's paintings.

Even though she'd already seen it when it was a work in progress, the canvas looked completely different hanging on the wall of the gallery.

Clare stepped back to assess the painting as a whole, then moved in to get a closer look.

In some of her paintings, Helen had left Theo's feathers perfectly intact. In others, she'd snipped, trimmed, even smeared them with color. But Clare could still make out their distinctive vanes, barbs, and hollow shafts. She tilted her head. "Mom?"

"Hmm?" said Helen, who was staring at the canvas with a rapturous look on her face.

"I don't know how you put so many different things

into your art." *Family, nature, love, sadness, hope.* "It's all in there, and it's really beautiful."

Helen kissed Clare's cheek. "Thanks," she whispered.

I wonder what the birds would say about their feathers being immortalized! thought Clare.

Grandma Lulu called out from the other side of the gallery. "Helen? Clare? We need you for a photograph. Hurry, darlings."

The photographer arranged the three of them in a row. She snapped a string of shots, the flash blinding Clare as if she'd looked at the sun for too long.

"Gosh, the three of you resemble each other so much," said the photographer.

When Clare could finally see again, she realized the photographer was right. Since her mom had completely grown out her red hair, she didn't just look more like Clare, she even looked more like Grandma Lulu.

Marisa rushed toward them. "The *Chicago Tribune* sent a photographer and a reporter, and they want to run a full-length feature on you, Helen. I can imagine the headline: '*Morrissey Artist and High School Teacher Discovers Her Inspiration in the Northwoods of Wisconsin.*'"

"It's all because of you, Marisa," said Helen. "If tonight is any sign of how smart you are, you and Mom are going to be *so* successful when you open your artist residency."

"You'll be buried in an avalanche of applications," said Clare.

"Bring it on," said Grandma Lulu, flexing her bicep like Abby.

"So many people have come up to me tonight, asking to buy your canvases, Helen." Marisa looked euphoric. "They're selling like hotcakes."

Clare couldn't believe how many people had arrived at the show. She watched them sip punch and eat dainty cucumber sandwiches. They moved from one painting to the next, looking closely at her mom's joyful explosions of color. Clare wondered what they were thinking. *Do they love the feathers as much as I do? What do they see in the grass, trees, and clouds? Do they catch a glimpse of themselves looking back?*

Another photographer approached. Marisa asked if he'd like to get a shot of Helen.

"Well, no," said the photographer. "Actually, I mean, sure. Of course." He turned as red as the tomatoes hanging from the Burches' tomato plant. "Her art is terrific, but I was hoping to get a picture of her daughter, too. It's not every day—actually, it's been never—that Mister Musky isn't a grown man but a . . . thirteen-year-old girl. And that Mister Musky hasn't just caught Alwyn's biggest musky but also . . . saved somebody's life."

It seemed to Clare that the photographer was trying very hard to appear at ease with this brand-new chapter in Musky Days' history. *Do not laugh!* she told herself, but she giggled anyway.

"I'm sorry," he said. "It's just a lot to get used to. Every year, Mister Musky is an older guy who's usually retired and has been fishing these lakes his whole life."

"I've been fishing these lakes my whole life, too," said Clare. "But I'm not retired."

"Of course not," he replied, fumbling with the strap of his camera. He took a picture of Clare and her mom and then slipped away, mopping his brow.

The door opened, and another group of people entered the gallery.

They just keep on coming and coming, thought Clare, happily. *And now it's time for me to get a cucumber sandwich—*

"CLARE BURCH!"

Clare stopped in her tracks. She would know those voices *anywhere*.

"Olive? Emmy?" she shrieked as she threw her arms around her two oldest friends. "What are you guys *doing* here?"

"Are you kidding? We wouldn't miss seeing you get crowned Mister Musky for anything—even a swim meet," said Emmy. "Our coaches set us free for the weekend."

"My dad drove us from Chicago. We're staying a few days at your cabin, and then Emmy's mom will pick us up and take us back home," said Olive. "We can't wait to catch all your candy during the parade tomorrow."

"Do my mom and Grandma Lulu know you're here?" asked Clare.

"Obviously," said Olive. "Who do you think invited us?"

How did any of them manage to keep this a secret? wondered Clare.

The door opened again, and the Porters walked in. Clare felt like her worlds were colliding. "Lola! Theo!" she shouted. "Come meet Olive and Emmy! Olive and Emmy, you *have* to meet Lola and Theo!"

Thirty-Six
And Now We Present

"This reminds me of what it was like right before you got married, Helen," said Grandma Lulu. "We were inside our house in Morrissey, while Henry and all the guests were in the backyard waiting for you to come out. You were positively *radiant*. We were fluffing your veil and making sure your bouquet of poppies and forget-me-nots was just right, and I was so nervous and emotional, and—"

"Sure, Mom. Except this time, we're in a bait shop in northern Wisconsin, and no one's actually getting married," said Helen. "Instead, your granddaughter is about to be crowned Mister Musky."

Clare rolled her eyes as Olive, Emmy, Lola, and Theo burst into laughter. She could even hear the Vogel brothers chuckle as they bustled around the bait shop, attending to last-minute details for the parade.

"Well, I feel nervous and emotional all over again," wailed Grandma Lulu. Out of habit, she reached out to pinch Clare's cheeks, even though Clare was as tan as a nut.

Helen glanced out the window. "There sure are a lot of people here. I'm glad Abby and Marisa grabbed a spot for us, right in front."

"I even see Jack out there," Lola whispered to Clare. "I can't believe he would have the nerve to show up after everything that's happened."

"I think Jack might be a lot be nicer than we gave him credit for," said Clare.

Lola gave her a funny look and shrugged.

"Mayor Bindlebauer will be standing behind the podium," said Bobb. "She'll welcome everyone, and then she'll put the Mister Musky sash and crown on you, Clare. After you climb into the convertible, the parade will begin."

"It sounds so official," said Grandma Lulu.

"You should know by now, Louise, that we don't mess around when it comes to muskies," said Nedd.

"There are bags of Rainbow Lollies in the convertible for you to toss out, Kitty-Clare," said Lloyd. "I know you love Caramel Dots, but Rainbow Lollies won't melt or make a mess in the heat."

"We've got a bag of Caramel Dots for you and your friends when the parade is over," said Bobb. "Just make sure to floss real good tonight. I don't want you getting tooth decay."

"Thanks," said Clare. "And of course I'll floss. I always do."

"We've got something else for you, sweetheart." Bobb picked up a large rectangular box from behind the counter.

"Why?" said Clare. "You've already given me so much."

"Open it," said Nedd.

Clare pried the cardboard open and pulled away the tissue paper. She gasped when she saw a fish—her musky!—nestled inside. She would recognize it anywhere.

"What?" she asked, cupping her cheeks. "How?"

"Remember the pictures your grandmother took after you caught it?" said Bobb.

Clare nodded.

"And remember how your mom measured her?"

Clare nodded again.

"We gave all that stuff to the local taxidermist, and he created a life-size replica," said Bobb.

"Good ol' Johnson," said Nedd.

"Best taxidermist in the whole county," said Lloyd.

"You guys technically aren't my grandfathers, but you're definitely the next best thing." Clare threw her arms around each of them and kissed their coarse cheeks.

"Aw, shucks," said Nedd.

"You're turning me into a leaky faucet, Kitty-Clare," said Lloyd. "Vogel brothers aren't supposed to cry during Musky Days."

"There's a first time for everything," said Bobb.

Helen dabbed her eyes. "If it's all right with you, Clare, we could hang your musky on the wall of the great room, between your grandfather's smallmouth bass and walleye—now that we're keeping the cabin, of course."

"I'd love that," said Clare. Before coming to the bait shop that morning, she and her four friends had pulled the purple *FOR SALE* sign right out of the ground. They'd left it lying in the grass for Juliet to pick up later.

Now, Olive, Emmy, Lola, and Theo were *ooh*-ing and *aah*-ing at the replica of the musky, admiring the rows and rows of needle-like teeth.

Grandma Lulu pulled Clare aside. "Something just came to me, darling. It's important."

"What is it?" said Clare.

"I've been thinking. Remember that line from *Charlotte's Web*? The one your grandfather underlined in his book? It said something like, 'It is deeply satisfying to win a prize in front of a lot of people.' We couldn't understand why it was important to him."

Clare felt the hairs on her arms stand on end. "Do you think . . . Do you think he somehow guessed what was going to happen? Did he wish it for himself? Or maybe even for me?"

"We'll never know," said Grandma Lulu. "But good glory, I need to go back and reread *Charlotte's Web* now."

He was my favorite person for so many reasons. Clare

hugged herself, and she felt her sturdy, beating heart. She knew he would always be there, right inside her.

Everyone had started talking louder. Clare could feel their collective energy escalating. She looked around the bait shop at each one of them. *I have so many favorite people now.*

"It's almost time," said Bobb, over the din.

Olive and Lola grabbed Clare's hands and escorted her toward the entrance of the bait shop. Emmy and Theo followed, chanting, "Mister Musky! Mister Musky!"

When they got to the door, Clare could hear the music and excitement beyond. She turned the knob, and warmth from the sundrenched front porch slipped inside and settled on her body. Mayor Bindlebauer's voice was thunderous through a microphone.

"And now we present . . ." the mayor was saying.

Clare pushed the door open. The bells on it jingled.

". . . *MISS* MUSKY!"

The daylight filled her eyes, and the cheering rang in her ears. She squared her shoulders and took a deep breath. Oxygen coursed through her veins.

As she stepped across the threshold, she welcomed the truth that had always been there.

I've had everything I ever needed.

It's been right inside me, all along.

Acknowledgements

My heart is filled with gratitude for the Original Six—Cindy, Dan, Elizabeth, Emily, and Anne Merritt—and for all the brothers, nephews, and nieces we've added into the mix. You are my foundation.

Endless thanks to my patient, encouraging, and insanely smart husband, Chip, and our three birdies—Caroline, Jane, and Owen—and to family near and far. In particular, I appreciate Auntie Susy, Uncle Bill, Aunt Tricia, Aunt Carrie, Uncle Mike, Aunt Sue, Aunt Judy, Aunt Mimi, Betsy, and Carol (the best librarian I know) for nurturing my love of words over countless years.

I owe an enormous debt to Mary Kole at Good Story Company for her close eye and editorial brilliance, and to Amy Bauer, for so many things, especially her mindfulness strategies.

My friends are everything to me, and I'll never be able to fully convey how much I love you all. Thanks for joining me on this incredible ride and showering me with support.

I salute the baristas at EVP Sequoya, who make excellent espresso and always provide me with a cozy place to write.

A huge shout-out goes to Jerry, Katie, Karla, Kim, Matt, Mike, Greta, Brian, Gary, Jeff, Jay, Joe, and their entire team for taking care of my favorite place in the world, which inspired the town of Alwyn.

Elliott Haberer, your enthusiasm for Clare has been the most precious gift!

Above all, I applaud Jeremy, Lauren, Kaeley, Veronica, Jenna, Sean, Natalie, Hannah, Jayden, and the amazing Shannon Ishizaki at Orange Hat Publishing. It's because of you that this book exists.

Hope is the thing with feathers.
—Emily Dickinson